TOUCH THE LIGHTNING

THE STORM BOYS SERIES
BOOK 3

N.R. WALKER

COPYRIGHT

Cover Art: Paper & Sage
Editor: Boho Edits
Publisher: BlueHeart Press
Touch the Lightning © 2023 N.R. Walker
Storm Boys Series © 2023 N.R. Walker

ALL RIGHTS RESERVED:

WARNING

Intended for an 18+ audience only. This book contains material that maybe offensive to some and is intended for a mature, adult audience. It contains graphic language, and adult situations.

TRADEMARKS:

All trademarks are the property of their respective owners.

AUTHOR NOTE

This series is strictly fiction. Actual bureaus of meteorology do not work like this in real life. The author is very aware.

There has been creative licence taken in regards to weather tracking, prediction systems, and any/all meteorological practices mentioned herein.

It's just a fun and crazy ride intended for entertainment purposes only. Please enjoy it for what it is.

Also please note with Australian English the plural for antenna is antennas, not antennae. We also use vice instead of vise, and further instead of farther.

For reference, Storm Boy and Mr Percival, as mentioned in this book, is from a much-loved Australian classic novel (by Colin Thiele, 1964) and movie (1976 and 2019).

Thank you for reading!

TOUCH THE LIGHTNING

N.R. WALKER

THE STORM BOYS
SERIES – BOOK THREE

BLURB

Without a working office, Jeremiah is tasked with repairing the automated weather station on Oxley Island. It's remote, only accessible by boat, and with there being a good chance of crocodiles, he's dreading it.

Tully, on the other hand, can't wait.

With a boat licence, his dad's boat, and two days alone with Jeremiah—and with thunderstorms likely—to Tully, it's another perfect adventure.

But their plans go awry when Jeremiah's research gets far too close for comfort. Thirty years ago, the day his life was touched by lightning, he was changed forever.

It's about to change again, only this time he's determined to set things right.

CHAPTER ONE
JEREMIAH

Twenty-three.

Twenty-three people had died in Cyclone Hazer, and a month later, I thought of them often.

Twenty-three.

A number I couldn't get out of my head.

Tully had told me I wasn't responsible for them, and the logical part of my brain knew he was right. "You saved countless more," he'd said. And he'd been patient with me, and he was kind and supportive. He was utterly perfect.

While I felt hopeless. And helpless.

I needed to work. I needed to get back into it and be productive. I needed to be functioning normally.

And my office was not functioning at all.

I had only a department-supplied laptop—since my own was fried from the electrical surge when we were at the bunker, and then of course with the cyclone—but I was grateful they'd sent me anything.

I'd added all the data I'd collected for my personal

reports. I'd collated stats and figures on heart rates during storms and the cyclone, from both my chest strap and watch. It was interesting, to say the least. And I'd collected more statistical analysis in my time here than I had in the few years prior.

But it wasn't work.

It was the longest time in my life when I hadn't been actively working, or studying for work, or doing something productive. I needed it.

So yes, the laptop was great, and it allowed me to stay in touch with the bureau and for me to watch radar loops for hours on end. But it wasn't enough to run the office.

All official bureau warnings for the Northern Territory were being run out of Queensland and Western Australia, and I had to wonder if they had any intention of ever re-opening the Darwin office at all.

Perhaps they were waiting for the media hype to have fully dissipated before they announced I was fired.

And there had been media hype.

Which was ridiculous. But yes, the blue-eyed weather guy—whose mother was the famous lightning-strike lady—had managed to send a warning message out via an old radar system by typing it over the office location sequence.

Well, there had been media hype across Australia, and even made news around the world, but not so much here in Darwin.

Given everyone was without power initially, then most news reports and updates pertained to health and safety information, it wasn't surprising my story got buried.

And I was glad it had been.

Tully's family knew, of course. He'd replayed the news footage a hundred times. And Doreen knew because she'd witnessed it.

But no one else gave a damn.

Thank God.

We had enough to worry about. Supermarkets were rationed, but we had power. Our phone lines were restored after a few days, and internet a few days after that. Many people were displaced, many people injured.

A death toll of twenty-three.

Twenty-three.

Twenty-three lives gone forever. Twenty-three holes where someone's loved one used to be.

It was an awful number.

A number I wasn't responsible for. I knew that. But still . . . it was a number I couldn't easily forget.

I also couldn't forget about how, during the middle of the cyclone, I'd had moments of disassociation. Full mental reasoning that the cyclone wasn't happening, that the deafening noise was no longer there.

That I could simply go out into it and risk the lives of everyone sheltering in the office to save a soaked and sodden bird.

A bird who, against all odds, was now thriving.

Mr Percival sat on the back of the couch, his favourite spot, and squawked for more food. We'd sought the advice from a local vet who provided us with more suitable dietary requirements that helped him learn how to feed on his own, and the little guy was growing so well.

He was losing the grey feathers, replaced with the more adult glossy black. He was curious and inquisitive and smart. He liked to perch on my shoulder and sleep against my neck when we watched TV.

Which was where we were when Tully and Ellis got home.

They'd been to work and then they'd had to sort out more insurance legalities for Ellis' house. As most people in Darwin after Cyclone Hazer were finding out, red tape and bureaucracy slowed everything down.

But at least Ellis was insured. Many folks weren't.

"How did it go?" I asked, not getting up.

Ellis threw a wad of papers onto the coffee table and then fell onto the couch. "Same shit, different day."

Tully came around and stopped when he saw me. "That bird is in my spot," he said. Then he came closer and gave Mr Percival a gentle stroke. "Lucky he's cute."

"He's getting better at flying," I said. "I think we should leave his cage on the patio with the cage door pinned open so he can come and go as he wants."

Tully's eyes met mine. "You want to get rid of him?"

"No." Mr Percival ruffled his feathers and decided to jump down to my leg, then across to Tully's leg, where he did his little hoppy dance on his thigh. "I want him to be happy and to be where he should be. Which is flying free with other magpies."

Tully gave me his puppy-dog eyes. "Aw, but you'll be sad."

I chuckled. "I'll survive. But he's not ready yet. He still needs help with eating those grubs."

Tully tried to stroke Mr Percival again, but Mr Percival pecked his finger instead. "Ow. That's not a worm, little guy."

Mr Percival decided to squawk and sing, just as Ellis' phone rang. He stood up and answered it as he took the stairs two at a time. Tully gave me a nudge. "He's been talking to Grace."

"His ex?"

Tully nodded. "He called around to see her after the cyclone, helped her with a bit of damage, tapin' up some windows or something. Anyway, there's been some texts and phone calls."

I had noticed him smiling at his phone lately. "Good," I said. "He deserves some happiness."

"He needs a good railing," Tully said flatly. "Might not be such a cranky fucker."

I snorted. He was so charming. "He just lost his house and everything in it. He's allowed to be somewhat cranky. Plus, he's living with you. His greatest agitator."

"I don't agitate him."

"You do. You're both as bad as each other."

Tully pouted and pretended to sulk. "Now I'm cranky."

I didn't bother with a reply. I knew what was coming.

He gave me the puppy eyes again. "You know what would make me feel a whole lot better?"

"I have a fair idea, yes."

He grinned. "A gold star."

I sighed. *And* there it was.

"Well, at least you didn't say a good railing."

"Oh, believe me," he said seriously. "There is a distinct correlation between the good railing and the gold star."

I laughed. "Is that right?"

He nodded without shame. "And I plan on getting both."

CHAPTER TWO
TULLY

I WASN'T KIDDING ABOUT THE CHART WITH GOLD STARS.

Jeremiah might have thought it was a joke at first, and he did laugh when I first showed him. But the time I only gave him a silver star instead of gold, he took it very personally and made his mission to earn gold stars every time.

Every.

Single.

Time.

And honestly, his performance was well above the silver star I'd given him, but his efforts since then?

Absolutely worth it.

I know people go on about sliced bread and penicillin, but I can declare, without a skerrick of doubt, the chest strap heart-rate monitor was the best invention ever.

Life had been pretty great, all things considered.

It'd been one month since Cyclone Hazer tore Darwin apart.

One month of living with Jeremiah. One month of learning more about each other. One month of adjusting. One month of watchin' him bond with Mr Percival, feedin' him, watchin' TV with him, talkin' to him.

One month of me fallin' more in love with Jeremiah than I ever thought possible.

The best one month of my life.

Not forgetting the one month of living with Ellis. Even that was fun. He gave me and Jeremiah as much space as he could, but even watching he and Jeremiah become friends made me happy.

It was also one month of disrupted essential services, disrupted food supplies, disrupted rebuilding. There'd been a lot of hard work by everyone, but things were slowly returning to normal.

Except for Jeremiah's office. It was still completely offline, but considering it required a full upgrade and fit out, it was hardly surprising.

But things like non-emergency medical tests were available—tests, like all the STI tests, for example. Tests, which meant Jeremiah and I were given the all-clear to ditch condoms.

Which was why, at midnight, I was face down on my bed with my arse in the air and the heart-rate monitor around my chest, gripping the bed covers and cussin' at Jeremiah to hurry the fuck up.

"I swear to god, Jeremiah, if you're not inside me in the next thirty seconds—"

"I am inside you," he mumbled, sliding his lubed fingers in and out.

I tried to get up onto my knees so I could turn

around and fucking argue, because his fingers were not what I meant and he knew it, but he shoved my head back down to the bed, his fist tight in my hair. "Stay down."

Oh, hell yes.

The ECG readings were going to be off the charts.

In contrast to the hair pulling, he ever so lightly ran his hands down my back and pressed his cock against my hole. "Are you sure you want this?"

"I swear to fucking Christ, Jeremiah," I bit out. "If you don't—"

And then he did.

He pushed his bare cock into me, slick and hot and oh so good. All the way in, in one long, slow push. His fingers dug into my skin and he made the hottest fucking sound. *A moan where pleasure is so good it dances with pain . . .*

"Oh fuck," he rasped out.

God, I love it when he swears . . .

The feel of him, skin on skin, knowing it was him inside me and nothin' else, no barrier between us, made me feel hot all over. It burned in my chest, the love I felt solidified into something more, something deeper.

He pushed all the way in, his hips flush against my arse, and he rolled his hips in that way he knew I loved. He stayed still, breathin' hard, before he pulled back a little and did it all over again.

He yanked my shoulder up, so I was on my knees, my back to his chest. And he held me like that, buried inside me, and he kissed my neck, my shoulder, his hands holding me, digging into me. But he groaned in frustration.

And then he pulled out.

"What's wrong?" I asked, confused.

He tapped my hip. "Roll over. I need to see your face."

I quickly obeyed, and he leaned over me, between my legs, and folded my knees up to my chest. And he kissed me, deep and slow, as he sank back inside me.

Oh god, yes.

This. This right here.

I wrapped my arms and legs around him, givin' him my whole body. He was so far inside me, his cock and his tongue, and it still wasn't close enough.

I wanted more.

I ached for it.

"Jeremiah," I whispered.

He groaned and shuddered, and with his forehead pressed to mine, his eyes imploring, he held still, strung tight. "Tully," he hissed. "I'm so close, I can't hold it. Tell me if you don't want this."

I slid my hand to his cheek. "Give it to me."

I could feel his cock twitch, impossibly hard and swollen and so deep inside me. His eyes rolled closed, and he thrust into me, driving upwards, and sweet mother of god . . .

I could feel it.

I could feel him come.

His whole body went rigid, his head pushed back, and the veins in his neck stood out. An animal sound ripped out from somewhere deep in his throat.

I could feel his whole body jerk and pulse as he spilled inside me.

I'd never felt anything like it. I'd never experienced anything like it.

I held his face and when he collapsed on top of me, his breath against my neck, I wrapped my arms around him and held him tight.

He was wracked with tremors, and he moaned as he began to pull out. I kept my legs around him, holdin' him right where he was. "Stay," I whispered.

I never wanted him to leave.

He pulled his head back, his eyes were glazed over and dreamy, and he kissed me. Open mouth, deep tongue, his face tilted so he could kiss me deeper still.

And he began to rock his hips, sliding his half-hard cock in and out, like he was trying to crawl into my body. Like he was tryin' to tell me something . . .

"Jeremiah," I murmured.

His gaze met mine, and his blue fire took me by surprise.

"You have my seed inside you," he breathed.

Jesus fucking Christ.

Wow.

His words heated my blood from my toes to my scalp.

I rarely knew what words would come out of his mouth, but I never expected him to say that.

He slowly pulled out and looked down between us. "And you haven't come yet."

"I don't need to," I replied. "What we just did . . ."

"I want you to do me," he said in a rush. "I want that."

Umm.

The fuck?

"Now?"

"Right now."

I was so stunned I couldn't speak. He'd once said that he'd bottom if it felt right, though we'd never explored that because I was a shameless, needy little slut who loved getting dicked.

Apparently.

He frowned. "Unless you don't want to . . ."

I flipped him over so fast he yelped in surprise, and I laughed. "I want to." I nudged his nose to mine. "Are you sure?"

He nodded. "Very."

Then, like he didn't need words to tell me what he wanted, he rolled over onto his front, spread his legs wide, and raised his arse a little.

I slid my hands up the back of his thighs to his arse cheeks. "You're so bossy."

"I expect gold stars," he mumbled into the sheet.

I laughed and leaned over him so I could whisper in his ear. "I can feel your come in me. You want mine in you?"

His breath caught and he stretched his back, raising his hips. But no, I wasn't lettin' him dictate this whole show. I held him down, pinning him, and grunted in his ear. "I will always give you what you want. Whatever it is, baby. I'll give it to you."

He writhed under my hold, unable to contain his need for it.

I knew how he felt. That give-it-to-me-before-I-die feeling. By the time I got him ready for me, his hands were fists in the bedding and his patience was worn thin.

His impatient whimpers and moans of pleadin' set my body on fire. Knowing I pulled his strings like a puppet . . . God, it was hot.

And then he growled.

I chuckled, because he sounded just like me.

Planting a hand by his head, I leaned over him and dragged my nose across the nape of his neck. "Patience is a virtue, Jeremiah."

He grunted, angry now. "Tully, if you intend to make me beg—"

I pressed the head of my cock against his hole and pushed in, his words catching in his throat.

Now, it had been a long time since I'd topped anyone, but it was never like this.

Never.

And it wasn't because I wasn't wearing a condom. It was because of him.

I ran my hands along his outstretched arms, kissing his shoulder and the back of his neck, and settled my weight on his back. I moved my hips slow, rolling and driving up into him.

I took my time, savourin' every second. Every heartbeat, every breath.

I wanted him to feel how much I loved him. I

wanted him to feel adored and cherished and how grateful I was that he was giving me this gift.

A gift he'd never given anyone else.

The fact I was inside him, unsheathed . . . he was so hot and tight, so perfect, it took every fibre of self-control I had to pace myself. I wanted it to last forever.

"I love you," I murmured, taking his ear between my lips.

He whined and threaded our fingers above his head, lifting his hips. "Tully, please."

"Are you sure you want this?"

He gasped and moaned on the exhale. "Yes, please, please."

So I let go of his hands and leaned up, my hands now pushing his shoulders into the mattress, and I began to thrust harder, deeper, longer. There was no going back, no stopping as I chased that peak of bliss, so close, so close . . .

My orgasm ripped through me, powerful and devastating, and so utterly perfect. Buried in him to the hilt, my cock surged and spilled, and he gasped as his body took every drop.

I collapsed on top of him, so wiped out and entirely boneless, I couldn't have moved, even if I'd wanted to.

I barely had the cognitive power to breathe.

I meant to close my eyes for just a second. I meant to rest for a minute and then get up and tend to him, make sure he was okay.

But the next thing I knew, it was morning.

His side of the bed was empty, and when I checked the time, I saw why. I'd slept straight through till seven o'clock, and he'd have been gone for an hour already. And I was sad, because I hadn't checked on him, I didn't know if he was okay. So I rolled out of bed, my body aching in the best of ways.

I grabbed my phone to send him a message when I saw he'd put the chart on my bedside table. I laughed, because there beside my name and last night's date was a very bright and shiny, big gold star.

CHAPTER THREE

JEREMIAH

Getting the bureau's office set up had been an ongoing nightmare. From supply issues to actually getting the gear delivered to Darwin had been delay after delay.

And don't even get me started on the actual install.

I understood all technicians, builders, and electricians were busy. Darwin needed a lot of repairs and rebuilds, and there had even been planeloads of qualified tradies coming in from various parts of Australia to help.

The response had been amazing.

But it was still frustrating.

One month later and I still had no working office.

I had spent one week at the Darwin airport, helping their control crew re-establish their weather station. It had been important work, fun and rewarding. Being productive and helping in desperate times—ensuring the city's only airport was functioning and safe—did more for my mental health in one week than all the years I'd worked in Melbourne had.

Helping the community, even in the small and non-concerting way I could, made me feel good.

It made the guilt a little easier to bear.

Guilt that wasn't rational, but guilt all the same.

But my god, I needed to work. I needed my office back. I needed to be doing something.

I'd cleaned out most of the old gear that was now in boxes. This whole office was going to be ripped apart, so anything that was worth keeping now sat in Tully's garage.

Admittedly, it wasn't much.

He kept the helmet with the light on it. For what purpose was anyone's guess. It was old and didn't work, but it made him happy, so . . .

A knock at the door startled me, and I looked up at the security screen—the only screen that still worked—and saw who it was. "Jememiah," a little voice said.

A little voice that made me smile.

I opened the door for Presley and Casey, the two little girls from down the road. The little girls I'd collected in a tackle-run to save from a lightning strike.

Presley, the younger of the two, called me Jememiah, and it was cute.

"Hello," I said. "Are you allowed to be up here?"

"Yes," Casey said. "Daddy's here with the roof man."

"Ah, good." I walked down the steps into the yard and, sure enough, saw Jeff talking with a few men who had a trailer of roofing iron. I gave him a wave, and the girls decided climbing into the Jeep was fun, and I didn't even mind.

That vehicle was indestructible, and if the wild pig tracks and potholes at the bunker or, indeed, a whole cyclone didn't break the car, two small girls wouldn't either.

It wasn't as if I had any work to do.

Then Arty from across the road came out with a plate of biscuits, the coloured wafer kind, and offered them to the girls and I. I asked him about his house and his cat, and we chatted a while. Jean and Michael were also doing well, and the couple across from Jeff were too.

And that was the thing about Darwin—the people who called it home.

Tough didn't begin to describe them.

Resilient and resourceful came to mind. Choosing to live in a city thousands of kilometres from any other city, plagued by insufferable heat and monsoons . . . it took a special breed of person to live here.

Like Tully and his family.

They took everything in stride. No problem was too big or too small. They supported each other and they worked hard. They supported their employees—some had lost their homes or cars—and the Larsons did everything they could to help them.

They were good people, and yes, despite having been on my own for so long, living with Tully *and* Ellis had been great. He and Tully bickered as often as they laughed, and despite the name-calling and frequent threats of homicide, they loved each other dearly.

I envied them all.

To have a family that loved as loud as they did was a beautiful thing.

I, on the other hand, had spoken to my father all of three times in the last month. And that included the day of the cyclone when Tully had held the phone to my ear, and the time when our lines were reconnected when he called to say he had seen my interview where I'd told him I was okay.

And once after that when I'd called him.

We'd never been particularly close, but it still stung.

Now that we lived at opposite ends of the country, the effort to stay in touch seemed too difficult. Maybe I hadn't realised just how much effort I'd put in when I'd lived in Melbourne. Or more to the point, just how little effort my father had put in.

I could see now that my relationship with my father was a thread stretched a little too thin.

Yet I didn't regret my move here.

In fact, perhaps it reinforced my resolve. I'd made the right decision to stay.

I'd never felt more loved in my whole life than I'd felt since I met Tully.

"You okay?" Jeff asked.

I hadn't even realised he'd walked up. "Oh yes. Sorry."

"M'girls not annoying ya, I hope."

"No, of course not. They're a joy."

He nodded to the office building. "How are the repairs coming along?"

"Slow."

He sighed. "Yeah. Same here. I got my place waterproof, so that's a start. But the roofing guys reckon they can start next week."

"Oh, that's great news."

Just then, a white Range Rover pulled into the yard and parked near the Jeep. Tully got out, and when Presley raced over to him, he collected her over his shoulder like he did with his nieces and nephews and put her in the backseat of the Jeep.

"Afternoon," Tully said to Jeff, giving me a smile instead of hello.

"A slow day at work?" I asked.

He groaned. "Busy as hell, actually."

"Which explains what you're doing here."

I noticed then just exactly what he had stuck on his collar. And he noticed me notice it, and he gave me that grin that sent the butterflies in my belly into a frenzy.

He was wearing the gold star I'd put on the stupid chart.

"I was comin' to take you out for lunch," Tully said. "Because I knew you wouldn't have eaten."

"Yeah, I gotta get these girls some lunch," Jeff said. "Good to see you both again. Hopefully we'll be neighbours again soon."

"I hope so too," I replied.

He rounded up his two kids, and as I watched them go, I could feel Tully's eyes on me and the smile he was aiming at me, waiting for me to look at him. "And I actually called around to see if you were okay after last night. I meant to treat you better last night, but I fell asleep. I didn't even hear you leave this mornin'."

I met his eyes. "I'm fine. What do you mean you meant to treat me better?"

He shrugged. "To care for you afterwards . . . you know."

Oh.

I pretended I wasn't blushing. "You treated me just fine, if you'll recall. You earned a gold sticker, did you not?"

He laughed and lifted his collar. "Sure did."

"Did you have to put it on your shirt?"

"Hell fuckin' yes, I did." He had exactly no shame. "I earned this."

I couldn't help but laugh. "You did."

He patted his collar. "And this isn't the sticker from the chart. I left it on there. This is a new one."

"Oh, so you think you deserved two gold stars?"

He looked me up and down and stepped in close. His eyes filled with a very familiar heat. "We can go inside your office and I can earn it again right now if you want."

"I thought you were offering lunch?"

"I am." He looked directly at my crotch. "I'm talking about an *actual* happy meal."

I snorted and gave him a shove. "You're so crude."

Then he winced and whispered. "I've had a semi all day. Ever since I woke up. I keep thinking about last night, you doin' me, me doin' you, and my dick hasn't quit since. Especially with the horse riding without saddles, if you know what I mean."

Horse riding without . . .

Oh.

Bareback.

I rolled my eyes.

He groaned. "Oh come on! You gotta admit, it was the hottest thing ever."

I couldn't believe he was talking about this—out the front of my work, of all places. Not that anyone could hear, but still . . .

I mean, what he said was true.

Tully laughed and wiggled in close. "Is that blush on your cheeks your answer? Is your face red because you're embarrassed? Or because it was the hottest thing ever?" He grinned. "Are you remembering how it felt?"

"Oh my god, stop it," I said, grabbing his arm and hauling him up the stairs and inside.

Of course he thought me manhandling him was a treat. He laughed and leaned his back against the useless radar console, offering himself. "You wanna do me again right now? Because you won't get a no outta me." He began to undo his fly. "Or do you just wanna little suck?"

The fact that my dick was half interested in that idea didn't help.

Jeez, what had I become?

I stepped in close, my fingers on the button of his pants. Because having a little suck sounded like a very good idea.

God, I was going to do this . . . in my office, during the day. Me, of all people.

I licked my lips and Tully groaned out a laugh. "Oh fuck yes. I was only joking, but if you're gonna get on your knees . . ."

Yes. Yes, I was going to.

Until my phone rang.

I saw the number on the screen and my heart almost stopped.

National head office.

All thoughts of fellatio were gone. God, I could hardly speak. "Tully."

"What's wrong?"

"What if they . . . ? Tully, they're going to tell me— I can't leave. I have too much work to do, and I have you."

The phone kept ringing.

And ringing.

Until it stopped.

"Jeremiah," Tully said. "What are you doing?"

"I'm not answering it."

"You have to."

"If I don't answer, they can't tell me to leave."

He was clearly confused. "Leave where?"

"Leave here."

"They're not gonna tell you to leave."

I gestured to the very dark dashboard. "It's not as if I can actually do any work."

"They didn't tell you to leave last time they called. You spent a week helping the airport weather-station crew."

"What else is there for me to do here? The repair team still haven't confirmed the ETA."

"Maybe that's what they were calling for."

Maybe.

Except I didn't think so.

My phone rang again. "Why did they have to fix the cellular network already?"

Tully snorted and picked up my phone, hit Answer, and held the phone to my ear.

I glowered at him and sighed. "Doctor Overton, Darwin office."

"Doctor Overton," a familiar voice said. Peter, manager of the national head office. "I trust you're well."

"Yes, thank you." I took the phone from Tully and put it on speakerphone, considering he could hear it anyway. "Any word on the refit? I'm hoping you have good news for me."

"Yes, and no."

"I'm not sure how news can be both, Peter. It really is more of an either/or situation." And I was betting on the bad news being what I'd been dreading.

Yet Tully's eyes were wide and hopeful.

And a little worried.

"Good news or bad news first?"

"I'd prefer neither, if I'm being frank."

"Good news first then."

I waited for him to continue, even though it became apparent he was expecting me to say something when I was not the one leading this conversation.

"Right then," he added. "So the refit of the Darwin office is scheduled and confirmed to begin the week after next."

"Oh, well, that *is* good news."

Tully's smile widened, and he nodded excitedly.

"We expect it will be a three-week job to complete."

"Okay." I wasn't sure what he expected me to say. "One week to start, three weeks to complete. That's reasonable."

"It's pretty good, actually. It's a complete refit; all new wiring and cabling has to happen first. You won't recognise your new office when you get back."

The relief I felt was visceral. They were fixing my office! And they weren't sending me away! But then I thought about what he'd said.

Uh . . .

"I'm sorry." My eyes narrowed at my phone. "When I get back from where?"

Tully was no longer smiling.

"When I get back from *where*?" I asked again, louder this time, when Peter still hadn't replied.

"Well, that's the bad news."

"Peter," I said flatly. "After the month we've had here, I have neither the patience nor the sense of humour for such games."

"The remote weather station at Oxley Island," he said. "As you know, we have a signal, but the radar system is offline. The local police said they could see by boat that the building is still standing but they don't have access to assess the damage. Might just need a simple reboot for all we know. And well, you're the closest manager on the ground . . . and you're not exactly busy right now."

The Oxley Island remote weather station.

Oxley Island was about three hundred kilometres from Darwin, situated off the northernmost tip of Arnhem Land. It was a small island with absolutely nothing on it but the automated weather station on the top eastern side. Which was, apparently, no more than a small, one-room brick building miles from anywhere and anyone.

The island itself had somehow escaped the direct path of Cyclone Hazer, but like most of the coastal parts of the Northern Territory, it had been hit by torrential rain and severe wind gusts. It just wasn't razed to the ground like some parts.

So, not too far away—certainly not across the country—but damn, it sure was remote.

"How long am I expected to be there?"

Tully was still staring at me, his eyes wide but now filled with more uncertainty.

"Well," Peter said. "We're trying to arrange transport. It'd be a full day's drive by four-wheel drive, and there *is* road access, but some of those roads have been damaged. Some are close to impassable if the last report was anything to go by."

Impassable roads in crocodile-infested Kakadu and Arnhem Land. "I know a thing or two about impassable roads out that way," I said flatly.

Tully grinned, nodding earnestly.

I glowered at him and shook my head.

Then Peter said, "And we'd still have to get you boated across from there. Honestly, it'd be quicker by boat from Darwin. But we'd have to find a local to get you over to the island."

"Boat?" I repeated. I was *not* a fan of boats, but the idea of driving more impassable roads along those swampy mangroves . . . I'd rather the boat.

"Whose boat?" Tully asked.

"I didn't realise this wasn't a private conversation," Peter said.

"Apologies," I said. "My . . . my boyfriend is here." I cringed at having to say that out loud. I still wasn't used to saying it at all.

Tully's grin was spectacular, and his eyebrows almost met his hairline. "Boyfriend," he mouthed.

I sighed.

I didn't call him that often enough, apparently.

"Oh, of course," Peter mumbled.

I didn't like his tone.

"To repeat my earlier question," I continued bluntly, "how long am I expected to be there? It's not exactly convenient to run to the supermarket from that location, so I will need to prepare many things, I suspect. And what about equipment? Do we know what equipment I'll even need to make repairs? If any of it is repairable at all, I should add. If the damage is structural, I won't be able to do anything. If it's a matter of replacing aerials or satellites, then I'm not sure how much use I'll be at all. I'm hardly qualified to install the equipment, Peter. Otherwise I'd have done my office by now."

"It's no longer connected to the mesonet. It could just be a connectivity issue," he said. "Or it might be a write-off. You could get there and do nothing more than fill in a damage report. Maybe nothing's salvageable. It's all old gear anyway."

I snorted. "You've seen the equipment list from the office I'm currently standing in, right? That all needs to be replaced. I can assure you, if the gear at Oxley Island is older than what's here, I'll bring it back to the Museum of Technology, Dark Ages exhibit."

Tully laughed.

"Yes, well," Peter mumbled. "Your office was long overdue for an upgrade."

He could say that again.

"Anyway," he continued. "We'd imagine the work itself at Oxley Island shouldn't take too long: a day, maybe two. But it's getting you there and bringing you back again that's proving difficult."

"If I'm going by boat, wouldn't the boat and the driver wait for me?" Surely they wouldn't drop me off and come back for me.

He made an uncertain sound. "Under normal circumstances, yes. But a lot of charter companies are out of commission with cyclone damage, as I'm sure you're aware."

"I'm aware, yes."

"I might even suggest maybe one of the news stations take you, and in lieu of payment, they could film you and the repairs, documentary style—"

"Absolutely not! I'd rather swim there in crocodile and jellyfish infested oceans than endure that special kind of hell."

Peter snorted. "Yeah, I figured you'd say that. It was just an option."

Tully gave me that gorgeous, insufferable smile. "Well, isn't it just as well that your boyfriend is the favouritest son of the owner of one of Australia's largest shipping companies? We happen to have boats."

"I can't take a cargo ship to Oxley Island," I replied. "Thanks anyway."

He laughed. "No, that's a ship, not a boat. But I do have a boat licence and access to a few different vessels. I can take you."

I stared at him. "You could take me?"

His eyes lit up when he grinned at me. "Abso-freak-ing-lutely."

Peter was quiet for a second. "Uh, was that offer legitimate? Because I'll need to lodge another permit."

Tully was so excited he was almost bouncing. "Hell yes, it was a legit offer." He patted his shirt collar and beamed. "I knew this gold star would be lucky today. How long can we stay for?"

CHAPTER FOUR
TULLY

It took two days for Jeremiah's and my permits to enter the Arnhem Land islands to come through. It took me that long to organise things at work, even though we were only expecting to be gone for maybe two days at the most, and it *was* a weekend. But my work had been busier than ever, and the days of the week hadn't really mattered since the cyclone.

Everyone worked every day.

But Mum and Dad knew everyone had been puttin' in long hours since Hazer, and they also knew I'd be goin' with Jeremiah whether I had approved time off or not.

He was goin' to a remote island, after all. A remote island that was only accessible by boat and was a true effort to get to—even more remote than the bunker.

There was no way I was letting him go alone.

My dad had two boats, and one in particular was ideal. A twenty-two-metre Sportfisher. It was designed for fishin', but it would be more than perfect for what we needed. Jeremiah thought the boat was fancy—and it was nice, don't get me wrong—but it wasn't the biggest or most expensive in its class. Not that I expected Jeremiah to know these things.

Dad loved his boat; he went deep-sea fishin' any chance he got. He *loved* it enough that he'd had it taken out of harm's way when the cyclone was due to hit. Like all the ships in our fleet. His fishing boat was no exception.

Growin' up, Dad had taken all his kids fishing, just like he took us hunting, and riding motorbikes, and camping in Kakadu.

Rowan preferred fishing. I preferred camping out at the bunker, and Zoe and Ellis preferred sports like football and CrossFit.

But we all learned how to drive a boat, like we all knew how to ride a motorbike or drive a forklift. Like we all knew how to cook, clean, and sew on a button.

So takin' Jeremiah to some remote weather station on an island for a day or two sounded like a holiday to me. In fact, I was secretly hoping for a two- or three-day stay. Albeit, he had a list of work he needed to do, and a crate of gear to do it with.

All I'd packed was a fishing rod, a change of shorts, and my toothbrush.

I wasn't expecting it to be all fun and games, but I got to tag along, help out, explore the area, maybe do a spot of fishin', and hang out with my most favouritest person. Not to mention the scorching hot ways we'd need to entertain ourselves at night, all by ourselves, alone with no television.

It was all a win for me.

The Bureau of Meteorology offered to pay me, and they did fulfil a bogus invoice I'd sent them. But I'd used the money they'd paid me for my 'charter service' to order a top of the range ergonomic desk chair for Jeremiah, because what they expected him to use wasn't good enough.

The cheaper one I'd bought him before, and Bruce the dog's chair, wouldn't cut it anymore for my Jeremiah.

Which I decided to tell him all about on the way to the marina when Ellis was driving us, because Jeremiah wouldn't be mad at me in front of my brother.

Or so I'd thought.

"Why would you do that?" Jeremiah said firmly. "You were supposed to use the money to cover costs and expenses for this trip."

"Because the chair I fixed for you before isn't good enough for the hours you put in. And the one you inherited when you took over is at least twenty years old, covered in dog hair, and has the impression of Doreen's backside in it," I argued. "And no doubt your head office would only approve basic cheap shit in the new refurb, and I want you to have only the best."

He narrowed those sharp blue eyes at me. "But now I feel bad. You're covering the costs of this trip—the fuel, the food . . . when you said you'd organise all that, I didn't expect you to pay for it. It was covered in the invoice."

"Sure. Honestly, the chair wasn't *that* expensive," I

countered. "But the way I look at it is that chair is technically for me as well."

He blinked. "You want to use my office chair?"

I winked at him. "Hell yes. I needed to ensure the chair was the best ergonomic design for spinal support, but also that it held both our body weights because we have to christen your new office."

Ellis laughed.

"Christen . . ." Jeremiah's eyes went wide when he realised what I meant. He glanced at Ellis, then cut me a rather sharp stare as he burned a spectacular shade of red. "Oh my god."

I just laughed. "Boats and ships are christened with smashing a champagne bottle before its maiden voyage. Office chairs should totally receive a similar bang and smash."

Ellis cracked up laughing. "Did you buy the chair from a sex shop? Because those are totally a thing."

I snorted. "No. But if you could send me a link, that'd be great. Gay edition, thanks."

Jeremiah sighed and turned to stare out the window, though the tips of his ears went red.

He was so damned cute.

And he was used to me and Ellis now.

Kind of.

"You still didn't have to waste the money on me," Jeremiah furthered. "The standard-issue office chair would have sufficed."

He was just mad that I'd used the money on him because he was only ever used to paying his own way. He'd had to save for every single thing in his life or go without, and me buying him things made him feel uncomfortable.

"Let him buy you stuff, Jem," Ellis said gently. He knew that Jeremiah struggled with anyone spending money on him for anything. "It makes up for his terrible sense of humour."

Jeremiah levelled him with a stare that said, in no uncertain terms, that Ellis and I shared identical senses of humour. Or maybe it was for the use of the nickname Jem. Rowan's youngest had called him that because they couldn't say his name, much like Presley and Casey who called him Jememiah.

It was cute when the kids said it, apparently. The adults, not so much.

I snorted. "Babe, if I kept the money for taking you to the island, it'd make me a real-life Julia Roberts in *Pretty Woman*."

He turned to squint at me. "What?"

So I explained. "You'd be paying me to stay with you and for the amazing sex we're gonna have," I said. "Which is technically prostitution. And we *will* be having a lot of amazing sex, because two or three days of just you and me and nothing else is a really long time. Now, I have no problem with prostitution or with role playing Julia Roberts if you wanna be Richard Gere. Or we can take it in turns with which one of us wants to be the pretty woman. I have zero problems with that."

Ellis laughed.

Jeremiah slow-blinked before sighing. "Your mind is a frightful place sometimes."

"I've been saying that for years," Ellis said as he pulled the car into a parking spot at the marina.

"You're both welcome." I got out and held Jeremiah's door for him. As he climbed out and when Ellis couldn't hear, I whispered, "I wanna be Julia first though, if that's okay?"

He smiled as I closed the door behind him, and Ellis already had the boot open.

"Hey, dickbag, come get your shit," Ellis said.

"Oh," Jeremiah said, rushing to help, but Ellis was clearly talking to me.

"You're not the dickbag, Jeremiah," Ellis corrected, shoving my duffle bag at me. He slid the black crate of gear closer. "This good to go?"

"I can take that," Jeremiah started. "It's rather heavy."

Ellis picked it up and began walking to the dock. Jeremiah shot me a he-doesn't-have-to-help-me look and I closed the boot and smiled at him. "You'll get used to it."

I would have thought he'd be used to it by now—having my family around so much, doing family stuff for him—but apparently not.

We followed Ellis down toward the dock where a familiar figure stood next to a gangplank.

"Morning," Dad said cheerfully as we got closer.

"Morning," I replied.

"Good morning," Jeremiah said. Ellis walked the crate onto the boat and disappeared inside. Then he looked at the boat. "Oh, good heavens, is this it?"

I knew he'd think it was too expensive or whatever. What could I say? My dad liked to go fishing. "Sure is."

He looked at it again, something on the roof making him look twice. "Is that a radome?"

I laughed. He was such a weather nerd. "Yes."

I even caught my dad trying not to smile. "It's a pulse compression radar," Dad said.

Jeremiah brightened. "Oh? What's the pulse repetition frequency?"

Dad beamed. "Up to five thousand nine hundred hertz."

Jeremiah was impressed, and honestly, I shouldn't have been surprised.

Then Mum appeared on the back deck of the boat. "Morning, boys."

"Hey, Mum."

"Hello, Mrs Larson," Jeremiah said with a smile.

"We've stocked your food for you," she said. "And Jeremiah, darling, I've told you to call me Brielle."

Jeremiah looked pained. It made me smile at him.

"And the tank's full," Dad added.

"You really didn't have to do that," Jeremiah tried.

Dad held his hand for Mum as she stepped off the gangplank, like he did every time. "Yes, we did," she said, giving Jeremiah's arm a squeeze. She understood that Jeremiah struggled with having a family that did things for each other and how it made him feel inadequate. He struggled with dealing with my large family most of the time, but he was trying to get past it. It just wasn't easy for him. Being alone, even with his father, it was so ingrained in him to be self-sufficient.

Many things were ingrained in him. Like his fierce independence and how showing any affection in front of others made him freeze. Whereas I came from a loving family that regularly hugged and told each other we loved them. He did not.

God forbid I ever bestowed the L-word on Jeremiah in front of my family.

He was okay when I told him I loved him now, when it was just us, of course. But no one else. Not even in front of Ellis.

I was still working on that.

Ellis came back over the gangplank and pretended to almost drop my car keys into the water below. He thought he was hilarious. "Very funny, nut sac," I said. "You break any part of my car, you pay for it."

"I won't break it," he said with a grin. "But I will drive through every red-light camera in town."

I put him in a headlock and tried to give him a noogie while Jeremiah talked to my parents. Ellis almost managed to junk-punch me so I let him go just in time to hear Jeremiah say, "I do appreciate it. When Tully told me you'd organised food for us, I worried we'd inconvenienced you."

Mum put her hand to his face. "Oh, you're such a sweetheart."

Oh no. She touched his arm *and* his face . . .

Jeremiah almost took an embarrassed step backwards off the dock. I shoved Ellis off me and went to Jeremiah, sliding my arm around his waist, making sure he didn't fall. "And that's enough scaring him for today, thanks, Mum."

Jesus. He adored my mother, and she had a real soft spot for him, but a compliment *and* a physical touch and a trip in a boat. He was going to need sedating.

He picked up his bag, pretending his face wasn't nuclear red and that he wasn't mortified, and he gave a worried glance at the boat and then to me. "And you assure me you can actually drive this boat. I'm not a fan of boats, as I'm sure I've mentioned. Several times."

"You'll be fine. And yes, I can drive a boat. Just like I drive the Jeep through Kakadu."

Jeremiah paled a little. "Oh joy."

Dad laughed. "Relax. I taught him everything he knows. He's very sensible. There's a satellite phone if you need, and there's also a flare gun. So if he drives irresponsibly or does anything stupid, shoot him with it."

Jeremiah looked at him, aghast.

"He's joking," Mum said, giving Dad a poke.

"Shoot him in the dick," Ellis said.

Mum whacked Ellis' arm but smiled at Jeremiah. "Ignore them."

"Why did you tell Jeremiah to ignore them," I asked her. "I'm the one they're telling him to shoot with a flare gun."

"They wouldn't actually shoot you, Tully," she said.

Ellis imitated holding a pistol. "It's really simple, Jeremiah. Just hold it away from your body, unlock the safety, and aim. At his junk."

I tried to push him off the dock. Fucker was stronger than he looked.

When I gave up and turned around, Jeremiah was

already on the boat. "Hey," I said. "I was going to help you across." I grabbed my bag and Jeremiah held out his hand to help me as I crossed the gangplank instead.

"Aww," Ellis cried. "Princess."

Dad shoved him for me.

I stepped into the boat, turned around, and flipped Ellis off. "It's *pretty woman* to you, nut sac."

Dad squinted, confused. Mum sighed. "I don't want to know."

"Thank you for everything," I said to them. "But we should head off if I'm going to get this handsome doctor to his destination before the tide changes."

Dad nodded. "Be careful. Call us if you need. Radio the coast guard if you get into trouble."

"Will do."

"Life jackets," Mum reminded us.

"Yes, Mum."

I took two life jackets and helped Jeremiah with his. I slipped it over his head and fastened the clips, cinching them in at his waist, making him jolt toward me. "Mmm," I hummed, low enough for only him to hear. "New kink unlocked."

He glanced over at my parents to see if they'd heard. They mighta done, given Ellis was grinning at us. Jeremiah shoved me away. "Thank you again," he said to my family. "Ellis, please look after Mr Percival for us."

He gave a salute. "Shall do. Just me and the bird all weekend."

"If you treated your girlfriends better, that wouldn't be the case. Maybe you'll treat Grace right this time," I said, then had to pull the gangplank onboard before he could cross it.

A few minutes later, we were unmoored and ready to go. Jeremiah was sitting down, gripping onto the seat under him as if his life depended on it. He was excited underneath the nerves, and I knew the best way to help with that was to put him to work. "Okay, Navigator, you're up."

He looked around as if I was speaking to someone else. "Um, what? I thought you said you could drive this thing?"

"I can."

"Then what do you need me for?"

"Just come up here."

He grimaced, and after considering his options for a few seconds, he came over to me. He was a bit wobbly, and this wasn't even the open sea yet. I had him stand in front of me, putting my arms around his waist to hold the throttle.

"This is all very high tech," he said. "This navigation system is better than anything in my office. Well, when I had a working office."

I pointed to the screen. He knew how to read this information. He knew maps and graphs and weather charts better than anyone. I took his hand and put it on the throttle, then his other on the wheel. "Okay, keep her under five until we clear the break wall. And see those buoy markers?"

He nodded.

"You gotta keep port side of those."

"What the hell is port side, Tully?" He cried. "Use terminology I understand."

"Left. Portside is left."

"Why didn't you just say that? Why does language change when you're on the water? That makes no sense."

"There's actually an etymological reason why nautical terms are used," I began.

"I don't care," he said. "Not right now. I'll care when I'm on solid ground and not driving a boat. Sorry."

I snorted. "Babe, you're doing great."

"You have more confidence in me than is warranted," he said, but after a while I could see just how much his cheeks were raised, how he was smiling.

"You can do anything you put your mind to."

He shook his head. Of course he'd disagree with me.

"You're driving a boat, Jeremiah."

He turned and grinned at me.

I grabbed the wheel. "Don't look at me. You gotta watch where you're going."

He pulled both hands away. "Oh. Sorry."

I kept him caged in my arms, my eyes on the bow. "We're gonna leave the shelter of the break wall here and go through Van Diemen's Gulf, up between the Tiwi and Vernon Islands, but from there we'll enter open water and skirt the coastline around Croker Island to Oxley Island," I said. "Read the navigation and tell me—"

"No thank you," he said, pushing my arm away and wobbling his way back to his seat. His hair was tousled by the wind and he looked so handsome in the sunlight. Even if he was holding on to his seat for dear life. "You said open water," he yelled over the sound of the engine. "That's where I opt out. Thank you for the offer though."

He was so adorable.

But I knew when not to push. He'd had a few minutes of fun, but he was clearly out of his comfort zone. And it was probably just as well, because crossing into open waters needed all my attention.

The gulf was spectacular today. The water calm and a magnificent array of blues and tropical greens.

It made Jeremiah's eyes stand out even more, dark sapphires against topaz.

I had to go over to him. I held his face up and smacked a kiss on his lips.

He pulled back in surprise. "What are you doing?"

"I just had to tell you you're beautiful."

He pointed to the helm. "Hold the wheel and watch where we're going. You can tell me I'm beautiful when we're on dry land."

I laughed and went back to the wheel, and he sat there and got all flustered and embarrassed, still holding onto the bottom of his seat with both hands. But he smiled as he took in the view. First of the Tiwi Islands and then the coastline as we made our way out to Oxley Island.

I knew he wasn't a fan of boats, but on a calm and sunny day like today—perfect boating conditions—he was enjoying it. Well, enjoyin' it as much as he could with both hands gripping onto his seat.

I'd imagine in rough seas it'd be a very different

story, but the water was as smooth as I'd seen it. The sun was bright, the warm breeze played with his hair, and I even caught him closing his eyes a few times as he smiled into the wind.

I wish I'd thought to take him out on the water before now.

But I knew I had a slim chance of ever gettin' him out here again, so I enjoyed it while I could.

I was disappointed it didn't take us longer to get there.

But as we came around the top of Oxley Island, I slowed right down and brought us in closer. I was assured there was an old jetty near the weather station that was still intact.

Another one of those things built to last, like the bunker, before red tape and a lack of common sense came in to play.

But given this jetty was wood and rusted bolts, I kinda wished common sense played a little bit harder. It was short and it did look robust. The pylons were as round as telegraph poles, which was probably exactly what they once were.

But it was still standing.

Kinda.

I lassoed a pylon and gave the rope to Jeremiah. "Pull us in," I said, going back to the wheel. He clearly hadn't expected me to get him to do that, bein' all wide-eyed and nervous, but like everything he did, he did it well.

I really loved how he just got in and had a go. Never said *oh, I can't do that* or panicked or whined about it.

He just used that big ol' brain of his to figure shit out and he did what needed doing.

I manoeuvred us in and cut the engine as he pulled the rope, and I tied it off.

"Be careful of the boards on the jetty," I said. "Actually, let me go first."

But it was too late. He threw the gangplank over and was already standing on the jetty by the time I'd finished speaking.

So impatient.

"Good heavens," he said, inspecting the wood. "Apparently they built this jetty when they brought the radar in by barge about twenty years ago." He looked at it, horrified. "How is this still even standing?"

"I'm surprised it wasn't washed away long ago." I walked across to meet him, and he held his hand out for me.

So sweet.

"Perhaps we should walk along the edge where the bolts are," he said. Then he grimaced. "Where *some* bolts still are."

"Yeah, how about we don't jinx it," I suggested. "Let's go and check out the weather station and see if there's anywhere to camp tonight. Or if we're sleeping on the boat."

With a nod, he led the way off the jetty and onto the wharf. It was a rocky platform, clearly man-made like Jeremiah had said, when they built the weather station and needed to offload gear. Further down was a small beach, dotted with large protruding boulders and rocks. There were a few palm trees, though it was mostly shrubs, and it was hard to tell if the cyclone had mown over them or if it always looked such a mess.

I was thinkin' it could be the latter.

But there, a few metres back into a clearing, with its own two-metre-tall fence built right around it, was the most prominent and probably only feature. There was a small, square, cinder-block building with a flat roof that appeared to be welded on. It reminded me of something from one of those worst-prisons-in-the-world episodes.

"Sweet mother of god," Jeremiah mumbled. He stood there, his arms by his side, his mouth open, and stared at the building. He shook his head, dismayed. "What even is this place?"

"I was just thinking it looked like a cell block, or maybe an outhouse at one of the world's worst prisons. Except for the mess of antennas and radars on top of it."

"Yes, well," he said as he opened the padlock on the gate. "This one is even older than my office."

Jesus.

Did he have any equipment that wasn't older than him?

I knew it made Jeremiah frustrated and disappointed, but it made me really fucking angry.

"If they don't upgrade you with all the newest and bestest of everything, Imma pay a little visit to the dipshits at the national head office."

He held the gate for me. "And who said chivalry was dead."

"Not me." I gave him my biggest grin. "I'm the most chivalrous man in all the lands."

"I'm certain cracking skulls and name-calling falls somewhat short of the chivalrous qualifiers." Then he smiled at me. "Though the sentiment is heartwarming."

I preened and he rolled his eyes before walking toward the building.

"Jeez," he said, now looking at something else in the corner of the yard. "Look at that."

There was a weather box on the ground.

Well, it used to be a weather box. One of those Stevenson-screen types, the white box with louvred slat sides. It was now on the ground against the security fencing in the far corner, half covered with branches and a palm frond. It was hard to tell if it was intact.

I went to clear off the debris, but Jeremiah stopped me.

"Leave it," he said. "For now. I'll need to take some photos first."

"Oh, sure. Good idea."

"Let's have a look inside the building."

"You mean the prison outhouse?"

He managed a smile. "Indeed."

We went to the door of the building, and he was getting the keys ready to unlock the old door.

"Wait," I said, this time stopping him. "There could be critters."

He looked to his feet. "What kind? Are there snakes here? On this tiny island? How did they get here?" Then his eyes almost bugged out of his head and he took a large step backwards. "Are there frogs here?"

"Truth be told, I'm not up to date on the exact eco-life of this island. I'd reckon, given the whole island is covered in these kinds of shrubs that seafaring birds are the main inhabitants. They're gonna take care of the snake and frog problem."

Okay, so some itty-bitty white lies to make him feel better weren't gonna hurt either of us.

"But I should probably just check, just in case."

He handed me the keys and took another step back.

The real truth was, I had no idea what could be in this shack. It didn't look like a human had been here in a few years, at least. But odds were there were other kinds of visitors. And probably the bitin' kind because, let's be real, most critters in the Territory were.

I picked up a fallen branch from a shrub and after opening the door, I nudged it open with my foot, holdin' the branch like a weapon. I'd rather a startled snake get a fang full of dried leaf than my leg, thanks.

But inside . . . there was nothing.

And I mean nothing.

Well, there were some old meters on the wall, like the real old electricity metres from the fifties or somethin'. There was a ladder propped against one wall, and there were swirls of undisturbed dirt on the concrete floor. Jeez, even the spiderwebs here and there looked abandoned.

Jeremiah peered in from the doorway. "I will never complain about my office again." He went in and looked at the meters, clearly tryin' to determine what they were for.

"How is this powered?" I asked. There sure as hell wasn't electricity here. "Solar?"

He nodded. "I guess there's a small panel on the

roof." He pointed to one meter that resembled a modem —if they had modems back in the 1970s. "That's a VSAT."

"A what?"

"A very small aperture terminal."

I snorted. "For real? That's what VSAT stands for? Clearly people who got to name shit lacked imagination."

He smiled. "It's a ground station for the satellite dish." Then he tapped the meter itself. "There should be lights, so the connection is broken between here and the satellite on the roof."

"Just a quick question," I said.

He turned to me, waiting.

I gestured to the meters and the room. "What the honest fuck?"

His eyes darted around the room, then back to me. "Uh . . . Was that your actual question?"

"I believe it was, yeah. Look at this shit." I gestured to the meters as if it explained everything.

He looked around and grimaced. "Well, I'm inclined to agree with you because . . ."

I snorted. "Because? Come on, say it, baby."

He smirked, but then dragged his finger across one of the meter screens and held it up to show me the reddish-brown evidence. "What the *honest* fuck?"

I laughed. "God, I love it when you swear. It's like you're being naughty." I waggled my eyebrows at him. "And I love it when you're naughty."

He rolled his eyes and sighed. "I know." Then he narrowed his eyes at me. "Baby."

Holy shit.

"Did you just . . . did you just call me baby? Like for real?"

"I was being sarcastic." He dusted his hands off on his shorts. "Because you call me that, and it's . . ."

I stared at him. "It's what? Don't you like it?"

"I know you're fond of it, but for me, it's unusual." He made a face. "I've never been called that by anyone, and it's not a term of endearment I would choose. If I had the choice."

"What would you choose?"

"Well, to be honest, I'm not sure I'd choose any term of endearment."

I gasped. "Why, baby?"

He gave me the stink eye, then sighed. "I don't know. Your name is already short, and your brother calls you Tull, which is sweet."

"You can call me Tull."

"But now it would feel forced."

God help me. How could he be so cute and so damn frustrating at the same time?

"You like it when the kids call you Jememiah," I said.

He pulled his bottom lip in between his teeth and shrugged one shoulder. "It's cute because they're children."

"Can I call you Jememiah?"

He squinted at me. "I seem to recall when we very first met that I introduced myself to you as Jeremy."

"But you're not a Jeremy," I said flatly, like *duh*. "You're a Jeremiah. Or a Jememiah. Or Doctor Overton.

Or baby. Or my personal favourite, which is 'fuck yes, right there.'" I panted. "Harder, harder, oh god."

He rolled his eyes. "You're insufferable."

I laughed. "Speaking of sex—thank you for bringing that up, by the way—I don't think we'll be sleeping in here tonight." I nodded to the concrete floor. "Boat sex it is then."

"I didn't bring it up."

"Shh. Do you want another silver star?"

He stared at me, then cracked up laughing. "You wouldn't dare!"

I took his arm and pulled him out the door. "Come on, let's take your photos. Then we can go explore the island a little bit before you suggest doin' something tragically boring like work."

CHAPTER FIVE
JEREMIAH

I AGREED TO GO EXPLORING THE ISLAND FOR TWO REASONS.

The first, so that afterwards Tully would allow me to get some work done in peace.

And the second was—given the size of the island, the lack of infrastructure, and the repetitive and somewhat destroyed vegetation—I figured it would take all of twenty minutes.

We began down the beach. It was rugged and mostly untouched. I'd hazard a guess that Tully and I were the only people to have set foot on the island in some time. It was small, barely two square kilometres, and sitting out in the Arafura Sea at the mercy of the elements. The island itself was mostly flat, and I could safely assume there was no elevation three metres above sea level. The vegetation, the shrubs and grasses were gnarled and ragged.

"Do you think the shrubs are this damaged from the cyclone?" I asked. "Or is this just how they look?"

Tully chuckled. "I wondered the same thing. This

eastern side was protected, somewhat, but I'd say this whole island cops it from all directions on the regular. My dad and his team use weather reports from here for their shipping routes." He made a face. "Well, they did. Before the cyclone. When I mentioned coming out here, he knew what I was talking about."

All the more reason to finish exploring and make some attempt at sourcing the problem.

I didn't say that. I just kept walking. I mean, how often would we ever get an entire island to ourselves?

"It appeared that old weather radar was still attached to the roof," I offered. "So I'd say there's just an internal miscommunication somewhere. Hopefully an easy fix. Not that I'm a technician by any stretch—"

Tully grabbed my arm. "Stop."

He was looking a few metres ahead, where the sand met the grass and shrubs. But his urgency had me on alert. "What is it?"

"See that?" He nodded ahead. "That track?"

It was a wide track of flattened sand with an odd divot, as if someone had dragged a zigzag with a stick right through the centre.

"I thought we were the only ones here," I said.

"We are." He took a few steps to get a closer look. "The only humans, anyway."

I looked at the track again, then shot him a panicked stare. "What made that? Tully, what animal made that track?"

He grinned. He actually grinned. "That's a croc. Big one too, by the looks of it."

A croc.

A freaking crocodile.

I took his arm in a death grip and dragged him backwards. "Get away from it, my god, Tully."

He was like an excited child. "No, look at how awesome it is! You can see where the tail—"

"No. No, immediately no. No, thank you." I looked at the scrub, then at the water, suddenly feeling very exposed. "We're going back to the building area that is fully fenced. Actually, now that I think about it, that fence wasn't built to keep people out, was it? It's to keep the crocodiles out. Good lord. Why wasn't that ever mentioned?"

He resisted my tugging him along until he relented with a laugh. "There's no crocs there now. They probably just come here to rest or lay eggs. So realistically, you're more likely to be surprised by one walking this close to the water's edge."

I may have screamed and jumped a good metre away from the water.

He snorted. "You just need a long stick. Kinda poke at 'em if you have to." Then he shrugged. "But honestly, if they're determined to get ya . . ."

I turned on my heel and walked back to the safety of the fenced yard. "I have work to do."

"Ah, babe, I was just kidding!"

"We need to have a serious conversation about your sense of humour."

He laughed again but fell into step beside me. "I'm sorry. No more croc jokes."

Once we got back behind the fenced area, I felt immediately better. Until I remembered that I needed my gear. "Well, shit."

"Well, shit what?"

"How do we get our stuff off the boat?"

He cocked his head. "Like you normally would. We walk on and carry it off."

"But there are crocodiles."

"Not on the jetty."

"But the jetty is unstable, and the waters are—"

He took my face in his hands. "Jeremiah, my love. I'd never let anything happen to you."

I rolled my eyes. "You won't let the already decrepit jetty fall away underneath me so the crocodiles can't eat me for lunch?"

"No, I will forbid it." Then he shrugged. "Plus, I'm the only one who gets to snack on you. Though now that you mention it, lunch is a really good idea."

I was so confused. "Are you talking about sex or actually eating lunch? It's hard to tell."

"I will always opt for sex. Always. But for the record, I wasn't talking about sex. But I am now. Because you brought it up." He grinned. "You have the best ideas. And I've never had boat sex before."

I sighed. "Work first."

"No, lunch first. For real." He patted his stomach. "I'm legit hungry. But then when we're on the boat—" He waggled his eyebrows and did some unruly hip thrusting movement. "—we should put that boat-rocking to good use."

I hated that he made me smile, and I hated that my dick liked the idea. I tried to be stern. "Lunch first."

His grin was spectacular. "This is the best day ever."

I snorted out a laugh. "Let's see if there are any crocs on the jetty before we rush into that statement."

There weren't, of course. But I kept an eye on the bay, giving a double look at every shadow in every ripple on the water. Yes, this small inlet was sheltered from the open sea, and I'd been thankful for that before.

Now I realised it just made it a prime location for crocodiles to come onto land.

We were both careful with every rickety and rotten plank on the jetty, and Tully held his hand out for me to step onto the boat. He pulled the Esky out and opened it.

"Let's see what goodies my mother packed for us," he said. He pulled out some wrapped bread rolls and handed them to me. "Ah, sweet chili chicken and Asian greens on a roll. Mum knows my favourite." Then he handed me a takeout container. "Dunno what's in that."

I opened it. "It's your mum's cold pasta and chorizo salad."

I'd mentioned once that I'd thoroughly enjoyed the cold pasta salad she'd made . . . and now she'd made it again.

He shook his head and kept rummaging, pulling out a second container of something different. I opened it to find cold roast chicken, all neatly sliced.

Tully sighed. "And this. Good lord, how long did she think we were going for?" He pulled out a bunch of bananas and then some bottled water. Then he grinned. "And look. A bag of the little Snickers."

It was absurd to me, and very foreign, that a parent would do such a thing as go to all this trouble and effort for their grown child. I could understand essential items —even my dad would probably do that—but never favourite foods and treats.

I doubted my father knew what my favourite food even was.

"I won't have to cook ya rice and spiced beef like I did at the bunker," he said.

"I really liked your rice and beef," I said, my voice quieter than I'd intended. "If I had to eat it forever, I'd still be grateful."

He looked at me then, a container of cut oranges in his hand forgotten. "Hey," he said with a frown. "You okay?"

I nodded. "Your mum spoils you. You're very lucky."

He slid the container of oranges onto the small table and took my hand. "I know how lucky I am. But honestly, this is more for you than me. Pretty sure if it was just me, I'd have gotten a Vegemite sandwich and an apple. Or maybe even told to get my own."

But still . . . "I mentioned to her once that I liked her salad. And the Moroccan roast chicken she did. And she made them again for us today. One time I mentioned them, Tully. Just once. And she did that for me."

He squeezed my hand and smiled. "She adores you, Jeremiah."

I had to swallow back unexpected tears.

"Oh, baby." He leaned over and rested his chin on my shoulder, softly kissing my cheek. "I'd say don't get too cocky about it," he joked. "Because she dotes on all her kids and their partners." He threaded our fingers. "But she knows you grew up without a mum, so I think she dotes on you a bit more than the others."

I nodded again, having to wipe away one foolish tear that had escaped. "My dad wouldn't even know what my favourite food is." I shook my head this time. "But that's not his fault. Growing up, I didn't really have a favourite. I was grateful for anything we had. Some things he cooked better than others, but I was still grateful. When I was old enough, I'd cook dinner for when he got home. Just simple things like mashed potato and sausages. He must have choked down some terrible cooking," I said with a teary laugh. "But he never complained."

Tully lifted our joined hands and kissed my knuckles. "What's your favourite food now? Of all the things you could have, what would you wish for?"

I smiled at him. "Rice and beef, a la house specialty of the bunker."

He laughed. "I'm being serious."

"I am being serious." I sighed and met his warm honey eyes. "Maybe it's the memories that go with it. Meeting you, chasing storms, and falling in love. And you cooking that every night. They're the best memories of my life."

Tully stared at me, really stared. A slow and shy smile tugged at his lips. "You just said the L-word."

I resisted groaning and I tried to pull my hand from his, but he gripped mine tighter. "No, no," he said. "No take backs, no returns. You said it. Let me savour this moment forever." He closed his eyes and inhaled deeply, then exhaled loudly. "There. Officially savoured."

I did roll my eyes that time. "Are you done?"

"Yep." He let go of my hand, but he leaned in for a kiss and waited for me to meet him halfway. Which I did, of course, and he smiled. "Thank you. I love you, and if you want spiced beef and rice any time, you just have to ask."

"I think I'd like it to be a bunker thing. Every time we go there, it can be our thing."

"You wanna go back?"

"Of course I do! I loved it. I wish we could have stayed longer. Perhaps next time we can. Weather permitting, of course."

He was practically buzzing with excitement, his eyes lit up, his grin wide. "Hell yes. Oh my god. I fucking love you. I love going to the bunker, and I love that you wanna go there with me." Then he got a far-off look in his eye. "You know, I wonder if I could convince my dad to buy a helicopter. I could get my licence and I could fly us in for weekends and stuff, and we could go all the time and—"

"Absolutely not."

"But then you wouldn't have to go down the mountain in the Jeep."

"Tully."

"Yeah?"

"Let's just eat lunch."

He repacked everything back into the Esky, sans the bread rolls and a bottle of water each. We ate in silence for a while, but I could tell by the furrow of his brow and thinking-while-chewing face that he was still mulling over the helicopter thing. "A helicopter would make—"

"No."

"But—"

"No buts. The Jeep is perfectly fine. More than fine. All discussions of helicopters are off the table."

I'd never heard of anything so ridiculous.

And expensive.

But mostly ridiculous.

He pouted as he chewed. "A fun boyfriend would say yes."

I snorted out a laugh. "A boyfriend who didn't care about frivolous spending or your safety would say yes. A real fun boyfriend would have packed the heart monitor strap to see if boat sex is a factor in varying results."

His eyes shot to mine. "Did you pack it?"

I smiled as I took a bite of my lunch. "I did. But which of us gets to wear it is the real question."

He laughed. "You're the funnest boyfriend ever. And just so you know, when we get home, I'm ordering a second one online so we can wear them at the same time. You know, purely for scientific purposes."

"Mm-hmm. Purely."

It took some convincing Tully that I should at least look at the weather box and radar on the roof before we retired to the boat for the evening.

"I get it," he'd griped. "Work comes before I come."

"No, before the crocodiles do," I'd countered. "I'm assuming they might like to come to land at dusk. I'd like to be on this boat before that happens."

And he couldn't really argue with that.

So back to the weather station we went. He held my hand this time as I stepped off the boat, smiling and pleased with himself for helping me the same way his dad had helped his mum.

But we carried my crate and gear to the cinder-block, cell-block outhouse, as Tully called it.

He wasn't exactly wrong.

The first task was to check the Stevenson-screen weather box. Tully made sure there were no uninvited critters using the box as a nest, and thankfully there weren't.

The box itself wasn't damaged, but the stand was well and truly broken. Inside the box, everything seemed to be intact. There were two glass minimum and max thermometers fixed to the back wall, plus three small remote sensors connected to the small hydrometer, a barometer, and a hygrometer, and I could only guess the reading units were in the cell block.

"Jesus H. Christ," Tully said. "How old is this?"

I shrugged. "I don't know. But the remote sensors can't be too old. And when I say *too old*, I mean not new, but not as old as my prehistoric Doppler in my office."

"I could order you a better system off eBay."

That was likely very true. "How's the stand?"

He righted the metal frame and it barely held its own weight. "I don't think we can fix it," he said, inspecting it. "Maybe I can rig something up, but it wouldn't last another big storm. Certainly not a cyclone. It needs a stronger base, anchored into a concrete bed."

"Mm," I said with a shrug. "I'm not sure if there's a point in even attempting to rig something up. Like you said, it needs to be done with the proper gear and equipment."

"And funding."

"Correct."

He inspected the box and the stand and sighed. "If we can get the sensors online again, then I'll try to fix the stand. If the box is dead, there's no point."

This was true. "Also correct. I should get up on the roof and inspect the damage to the antennas and satellite dish."

Tully carried out the ladder and held it for me while I climbed up. As soon as I could see on top, I could see what was wrong. There were several antennas, two were now laying on the far edge, only attached by wires, and the tracking satellite dish was damaged. "The LNB is disconnected," I said, climbing up the last rung and lifting myself onto the roof.

"The low-noise block?" Tully asked. "Please be careful up there."

"This roof is a lot sturdier than the jetty," I said. "And yes, the LNB has completely come off the feed arm. I should be able to reattach it. But some antennas are down."

I took a bunch of photos with my phone before trying to fix the LNB, but it wasn't as simple as just reattaching it. The port jack was broken off inside it. "I don't think the noise block is repairable," I said, loud enough for Tully to hear. "But the antennas might be. They're still here, at least." I walked to the edge so I could see Tully. "Remember how you MacGyvered the booster at the bunker? These antennas might just need MacGyvering."

"Okay, I'll come up, hang on."

"Let me get down first." I climbed down and showed him the photos, and with a nod, he grabbed a few tools before he went up.

Did I find it extremely attractive that he was so handy?

Yes.

Was the fact he could fix things a turn on for me?

I was beginning to think it might be.

"You know," I said, "there's a lot to be said about the sexy handyman persona. A man who can use tools and isn't afraid to get his hands dirty. I never realised I had a thing for such appeal."

Tully's smiling face appeared. "You okay down there?"

It didn't help that he was holding a pair of pliers.

"I'm great. How are you up there?"

He laughed and snapped the pliers. "Do you have a fetish I didn't know about?"

"I wouldn't call it a fetish," I argued, thankful we were all alone on this island. "But if you were to also perhaps look at purchasing a tool belt, I wouldn't be mad about it."

He laughed. "Would I get extra gold stars?"

I pretended to have to consider this. "Hmm, maybe. Would you be naked under that tool belt?"

"I can be naked right now," he said, pulling his T-shirt over his head. He threw it down to me, and by some miracle, I caught it.

"Keep your shorts on. I don't think dangling your bits on that hot tin roof will do either of us any favours."

He burst out laughing. "But then you'd get to kiss them better."

I snorted. "What difference does that make when you know I'll kiss them anyway? You don't need to put yourself through what I would imagine is a rather excruciating lesson."

He grinned. "I'll hold you to that."

"I don't doubt you will."

He was still grinning. "Want me to come down now and you fulfil your promise, or should I fix your antenna first?"

"Antenna, please."

He sighed. "So cruel."

But he disappeared from view, and after a few moments, I decided to climb up and watch him from the ladder.

Until he tried to kneel on the roof and hissed at how hot it was. "Here," I said, throwing his shirt back to him. "Kneel on that."

He was very obviously surprised to see me peering at him through the top two rungs of the ladder. "Are you perving on me?"

"It's not perving," I replied. "Think of me as the

OH&S officer in this working agreement. I'm supervising."

He laughed, but he shoved the shirt under his knee and went about fixing the antenna. He had a cordless drill and some screws and had it fixed again in no time. "The backing plate's a bit bent, but she'll be right," he said. "Now, if you wouldn't mind supervising from inside and see if anything's back online."

Oh, yes. That's probably a good idea . . .

Except there was no change, no miraculous fix. Everything was still dead.

"Nothing," I yelled.

"Let me see if I can fix the satellite thing," he replied.

I went back out and up the ladder to watch him again. He was standing now, shirtless in the sunshine, his muscular torso glistening with sweat, his hair being tousled in the wind. How, in this lifetime, this man was in love with me, I would never know.

But for some ridiculous reason, he was. I knew this fact all too well because he told me, with his whole chest, at least once a day.

I wished I could say it back to him. I wished I could be so carefree with my declarations of affection, but every time I tried, the words wouldn't come out.

I wanted to tell him as often and with my whole heart the way he told me.

But still, I couldn't.

It was fear that stopped me. Fear of putting myself out there—which was stupid because I was already well and truly out there for him. It was fear of being exposed and admitting my vulnerability.

And that was probably the biggest difference between Tully and me.

I grew up believing that to show any emotion was a sign of weakness.

Tully grew up believing that love was the ultimate strength.

"Whatcha lookin' at?"

I blinked in surprise and grabbed the ladder I forgot I was standing on. I'd totally spaced out.

"I was looking at you," I said. "I just got distracted."

"Picturin' the totally hot boat sex we're gonna have, huh?"

"Something like that."

"How about you do your boat-sex daydreamin' on the ground?" He had the broken jack port in his hand. "I'd rather you didn't fall."

"I'm fine," I said. "I have hold of the ladder. But the wind is picking up. Perhaps you could get down off the roof too."

"Let me just see if I can salvage this," he said. He was holding the end of the LNB, trying to extract the broken jack, trying to reattach the broken pieces together. "Would electrical tape fix this?"

"I highly doubt that. I think it's a replacement job."

"Did they send you a new one of these noise things?"

"A low-noise block? No, they did not. They didn't send me much of anything."

He grumbled about that, but reassembled the jack into the port, trying to get a reconnection. "It really just needs a new connection. It's the little prongs that are bent, see?" He held it out to show me. "Unless it snapped the internal wiring. Then it's a replacement job."

He was so clever. So inquisitive, and—

"Are you picturing me with a tool belt again?" He was grinning at me.

"Possibly."

"Wanna check the meter things?"

"Yes, of course."

I climbed down the ladder and went back inside, but nothing was spinning, nothing was flashing. "No change," I yelled.

"Hang on," he called out. "How about now?"

A green light, faint as could be, flickered, then died. "Wait! What did you do? Do it again!"

A second later, the same green light flickered on, stayed green for half a second, then died again. "Yes, that!" I said. I went outside so I could speak up to him. "There was a brief green light on the tracking sensor. It comes on for a second, then goes off. So there's some kind of signal."

"Okay, let me try again," he said.

It took a few attempts, some disassembling and reassembling and some electrical tape, but he managed to get one green light to stay on. "Hold it there," I yelled, excitedly. "We have one solid green light."

"Awesome!" he said, tossing his shirt down to me, then climbed down the ladder. As soon as his feet were on the ground, I gave him a kiss, then pulled him into the room.

"Look!" I showed him the single green light. "You did that."

His smile faded as he stared at the old white box. "But there should be four," he said.

"Well, yes. But even one light tells us that there's a connection."

"But why aren't all the lights on?"

"I'd say there's a connectivity issue with the wiring. And that's a job for a technician."

"Lemme see if I can do somethin' with those antennas."

Back up he went, and after some MacGyvering with the antenna and aerials and securing the bases, he had them all upright at least.

I watched the different sensor units, not holding out much hope but excited all the same.

"How's that?" he yelled.

"Nothing."

There was more grumbling from the roof. "Okay, what about now?"

"No." But then another sensor light blinked on. "Wait! Yes, right there!"

"Right there, baby. Yes, yes," he yelled in a provocative tone.

And another sensor came on.

"There! You got another one."

But after some more cussing and sighing, the last one wouldn't come on. All up, three out of five was better odds than I could have hoped for.

When Tully climbed down off the ladder, I pulled him inside again. "Look at what you did!"

He smiled. "I'm pissed about the last two."

"I'm not. This place needs a full upgrade and install. We fixed more than we rightly should have. If all we'd done was come here and taken some photos and filled in a damage report, I'd still call it a success. But we have readings." I couldn't help feeling a little proud. "There better be some happy people in head office."

Tully laughed. "There better be, yes. You can tell them that your boyfriend did a super impressive job, and we'll just keep the fact that between you and me that all I really did was jiggle some wires and screwed a few antennas back into place."

"Believe me, I'll be telling them exactly everything you did."

"I took some photos for your report," he said, showing me on his phone. "But now I guess we better try and fix that box stand, or the readings sent back to head office won't be correct."

This was true. Stevenson-screen weather boxes had specific location and height requirements to achieve the most accurate results.

"It's gotta face south, right?"

"That's correct. How do you know that?"

He made a face as we went back outside. "I'm a storm guy, remember? And we made one in high school for science class."

He carried the box over to where the stand had broken off at the ground, then took his shirt from where he'd tucked it into the back of his shorts and wiped his face with it.

"Ugh, it's gettin' hot," he said, and immediately we both looked up at the sky.

There were dark clouds coming in from the west. Cumulus, low and dark.

Storm clouds.

Our eyes met, and he grinned.

CHAPTER SIX

TULLY

AS SOON AS JEREMIAH'S GAZE WENT FROM THE INCOMING storm to me, we both smiled.

An incoming storm while we were on some remote island, without another single person for miles, could only mean one thing.

And bein' so far from anywhere, with no internet or nothin', we had no idea how long this storm would last, how deep the trough was, or how good or bad it was going to get.

"I say to hell with the stupid weather box," I said. "Time for awesome boat sex."

He checked his watch with a smirk. "Well, it is getting on in the afternoon." Then he looked out to the water and his smile died. "And I'd rather be on the boat before any crocodiles decide to take shelter on land."

"Solid plan."

He closed the door to the cell block, left the box right where it was, and pulled the gate closed. And it wasn't until he crossed the jetty to the boat that something occurred to him.

"Oh my," he said, his arms out for balance. "The boat . . . the turbulence . . ."

I laughed. "Uh, it's not called turbulence on a boat," I said, jumpin' in beside him and holding onto him. "The seas get choppy in storms. You know this. You issue weather warnings for sea swells all the time, do you not?"

"Well, yes," he said, gripping onto the doorframe into the cabin. "Theoretically, I'm well aware, thank you. But in practice, I'm never on a boat. My god, Tully, is this even safe? Should we leave?"

I bit back my smile because he was clearly stressing. "Babe, we'll be fine. We're securely moored, and this boat is designed for these conditions."

And the truth was, this wasn't even choppy yet. But I didn't tell him that. He was already a little pale.

"How about we get you into the cabin?"

"Good idea."

I got him situated and closed the door, and he relaxed immediately. But as the skies grew darker and the boat began to rock a little more, his grip on the seat cushion tightened.

"Want something to eat?" I suggested.

He grimaced. "Probably not."

"Some water?"

He shook his head, and his knuckles were now white.

I was beginning to think that our awesome boat sex was probably out of the question.

"Okay," I murmured, peeling his fingers free of the seat. He transferred the death grip to me instead. "Um, ouch."

He looked at our hands. "Sorry."

"Would you like me to show you the radar," I said, pointing at the screen. "And you can see the storm, see the numbers and stats, and you'll know that you'll be okay."

He shook his head again, his mouth a thin line. "It's not the storm."

Ah, damn.

"Jeremiah, you'll be fine. You're with me."

He nodded.

"I know you don't like boats."

"Well, technically, it's probably not so much the boat as it is the crocodile-infested water the boat is currently bobbing up and down in."

"Would you feel safer if we headed out?"

His eyes shot to mine. "But you said this inlet is protected against the wind, and I therefore assume the storm."

"That's true."

"So, which is worse? Open sea in a storm, or a partially protected inlet which may or may not be home to crocodiles?"

"Well . . ."

Don't tell him crocodiles also exist in the open sea. Don't tell him that. Don't say it.

"Oh my god, there are crocodiles everywhere, aren't there?"

"Not technically everywhere."

"For the love of all that is holy."

My knuckles were starting to grind. "Can we lessen the death grip? Because, ow."

He released my hand from his vice-like grip. "Sorry."

"Would you feel better if you wore a life jacket?"

He made a face. "Not particularly." Then he seemed to reconsider. "Maybe."

"Let me get it for you."

"And you. I'd feel a lot better if you wore one too."

"Okay."

Yep. Awesome boat sex was well and truly out of the question.

I helped him into his vest and clipped mine on, and he did seem to breathe a little easier. But then thunder rumbled overhead.

"I think this will be the first storm I've not actually enjoyed," he said. Both his hands were balled into fists on his lap.

I sighed and took his hand, trying to unfurl his fingers. There was only one way to help him, and that was distraction.

"When you went to South America to see the Catatumbo storms for your thesis studies, did you go on any boats then?"

"Yes."

"And did you not experience any storms when you were on a boat?"

He blinked a few times. "I think so, yes."

"And were you this worried then?"

"Not that I remember." Then he looked at me,

annoyed. "And I know what you're thinking. That it's foolish that I'm worried now."

"I would never think it's foolish."

"Then why did you bring it up?"

"I just thought I'd point out that you were fine back then, and you'll be fine now."

"But I didn't have you then."

"What difference does that make?"

"Because."

"Because why?"

"Because I'm worried for you."

"Are you saying you love me? I'm pretty sure you're saying you love me."

He rolled his eyes, but his grip on my hand had lessened somewhat. "Are you trying to distract me?"

I laughed. "Yes. And it's working. Because I'm getting some feeling back in my pinky finger."

He let go of my hand completely. "Sorry."

"Don't apologise." I shrugged. "If that didn't work, I was going to suggest throwing these seat cushions on the floor and distracting you in carnal ways."

He almost smiled, until thunder rumbled overhead, louder this time.

Closer.

He grabbed my hand, and his grip was vice-like again. "Does this boat have lightning rods?"

"Yep. It has—"

"Good."

I noticed then that he was doing that mouth thing, where it tasted bad, and sure enough, lightning cracked and lit up the sky.

"We'll be fine," I whispered, but the boat rocked more, the water slapping the hull.

"What's that noise?"

"It's just water."

"It's not a crocodile testing the structural integrity of the hull?"

I snorted. "No. This isn't *Jaws*."

Which was the very wrongest thing I could have ever said because his eyeballs almost exploded out of his head. "Sharks? Oh my god, Tully, why would you say that?"

I had to prise my hand from his death grip before he actually broke some bones. "I realise now that I shouldn't have said that."

He really wasn't having a good time.

The thing was, this was a purpose-built fishing boat. It wasn't built for comfort, per se. I mean, it was very comfortable, but it was no luxury yacht with full-length beds. It was built for fishing. And given we were both wearing life vests, we wouldn't fit together if we lay on the bench seat. Our cuddle room was limited.

"Okay, stand up," I said, getting to my feet.

He did so, reluctantly. "Why?"

I pulled the thin seat cushions off the seats and laid them on the floor, then unrolled a sleeping bag, unzipping it so it was more like a blanket. "Lie down," I said, sitting on the floor. I waited for him to join me and then I spread the blanket out over us.

I pulled him into my arms, his head on my biceps, and despite the life-vest situation, I held him the best I could.

Rain pelted the windows and we rocked as thunder rumbled overhead. But he breathed deeper and the tension in his body began to melt away.

"Feel better?"

"Yes. Much."

I patted his head, rubbed his arm, and hooked my leg over his as the boat rocked and the storm raged.

"Enjoying the storm now?"

"Not particularly. I mean, this is nice. And I appreciate you accommodating me."

I wanted to laugh but thought better of it. "I'm not accommodating you." I kissed the side of his head. "You say it like it's a chore or an obligation. I want you to feel safe. I don't like it when you're scared, baby. I'll do anything to make you feel better."

Thunder boomed and the sky lit up with a crack of lightning, but he buried his face in my armpit. "We're missing a really good storm, babe."

He pulled his head back and risked a look upward until he made a dry heaving sound. "Ugh, why is the sky moving like that?"

I chuckled and tucked him back into my side. "It's the boat that's moving. Not the sky."

"Please don't talk about it," he mumbled.

"Sorry."

We were quiet again while the rain lashed at the windows and the waves rocked us. It was probably louder inside the cabin, truth be told, but we were warm, dry, and we had each other.

"We should have brought a tent," Jeremiah said. "We could have set it up inside the fenced area."

"We'll do that next time."

He laughed, and maybe, just maybe, he sounded a little crazy. "There will be no next time. I'm never getting on another boat, sorry."

"Not ever?"

"I like terra firma, thanks all the same. And if head office ever suggests I come back here, I'll be explaining my *hell no* in great detail."

I laughed. "Will there be expletives?"

"Most likely."

I patted his hair down on the back of his head and kissed his forehead. This distraction ploy was working a treat. I had to keep it going. "Okay, super-serious question time."

"Is it about sex?"

"No."

"Then, yes?"

"If it was about sex, would you not answer?"

"I'd answer, yes. But if the question was a proposition or suggestion to partake in sex right now, then my answer would be no."

I snorted out a laugh. "That wasn't my question."

"Then ask away."

"If I were a breed of dog, what would I be?"

He froze. "What?"

"If I were a breed of dog, what breed would I be?"

"What kind of question is that?"

"A very serious and important kind of question."

He was quiet for a second. "A golden retriever. Shaggy blond hair, cutest smile, big brown eyes, kindest heart. The very goodest of boys."

I laughed. "Sounds like you're a bit fond of me."

He smacked my arm. "Oh shush. What kind of dog would I be?"

I sighed, long and loud. "What's the smartest breed?"

"I'm not entirely sure. Alsatians rank high, I believe."

"Like a police dog? *No*, you're more of a border collie."

"Are you saying I herd sheep?"

I laughed. "No. Ooh, I know. You're a kelpie. Smart as hell, analytical thinker, can be savage if you need to be."

"But I'm still herding sheep."

"And if I were a cat, what kind of cat would I be?"

"One that can run fast because, if I'm still a kelpie—"

I burst out laughing. "No interspecies breeding allowed."

"Oh my god, Tully. Why would your brain even go there?"

"Okay, next question, if we were to wake up tomorrow as a different species, would you still love me?"

"Well, yes, though there would be many varying factors. And so you're aware, love doesn't equal sex, and sex doesn't equal love. They're not mutually exclusive, you know."

"I know. But you still didn't answer. What are the varying factors?"

"It would depend on the difference in species. Are

they compatible in any way, or are they natural born enemies?"

"Okay, you're *way* overthinking this. It was really just a simple yes answer."

"Then yes."

"But what if I were a frog?"

He shuddered. "Then no. Sorry. You're on your own."

I laughed and pulled his face back to kiss him. "You absolutely would still love me."

"Not if you had suction cups for feet. I absolutely would not." He shuddered.

I laughed again, and his gaze went up to the roof. To the gentle splatter of rain, the grey skies that were no longer moving so much.

"Uh, I think the storm is over," he whispered. "The boat's no longer bobbing like a cork."

I smiled at him, unwrapped my leg from his, and stroked his hair. "You okay now?"

"Your art of distraction game is strong. Thank you. I freaked out, sorry."

I kissed him. "Don't apologise. The first time on a boat in a storm is scary for anyone." I sat up, my back against the seat, and he did the same opposite me, his leg resting against mine. "Are you hungry now? It's getting late."

"A little."

I leaned over and pulled the Esky closer. "Mum's pasta salad sound good?"

"Perfect."

With the container between us and armed with a fork each, we managed to demolish half of it.

"So, can we discuss the if-I-was-a-frog thing?" I asked. "Because you're supposed to be my prince charming, which means you're supposed to kiss the frog to turn me into a real boy."

"I think the real-boy storyline is Pinocchio."

I shrugged. "Sentiment is the same."

"Any other animal but a frog."

"A slug?"

"Fine."

I grinned at him. "I'd kiss you no matter what animal you were. Even if you were a face-eating lion. I'd risk it."

"Valiant, but foolish."

"Thanks."

He shoved a forkful of pasta into his mouth and spoke around it. "What about a praying mantis?"

"I dunno. Do they speak with their mouth full?"

He laughed and swallowed it down. "I can't be certain. But they do rip off their mate's head after copulation."

I stabbed some pasta and sausage. "Are you having psychotic tendencies I should know about?"

He smiled. "No. But I'm having copulation tendencies. After you were so very kind and sweet to distract me when I thought we were about to be croc food. I was thinking I could show you my gratitude."

I grinned at him. "Copulation tendencies and gratitude are my three favourite words."

He took the container and our forks and slid them

onto the seat behind him, then straddled my thighs. "I am very grateful for the way you look after me," he said, tilting my chin up and kissing my lips. "And I spent all day admiring your body and your muscles and how capable you are."

"I'm definitely buying a tool belt when we get home."

He chuckled and undid my life vest, one slow clip at a time. I was more rushed with his, unclipping it and sliding it over his shoulders, momentarily restraining his arms at his sides and pulling him down for a hard kiss.

His eyes flashed with blue fire, and I laughed . . .

Until he slid his hand around the back of my head, pulled my hair so my face angled upwards, and he kissed me. Teeth, tongue, slowly grinding his hips, seeking friction.

I gripped his arse, pulling him down as I drove my hips up to meet him. He grunted, the most obscene sound, and he deepened the kiss.

I dug my fingers into his arse cheeks and realised . . . he wasn't wearing underwear. Again.

My god, this man.

Commando really was my favourite thing.

I flipped him over onto his back on the cushions on the floor and kissed him again, settling my weight between his legs. He brought his knees up, his hands on my arse, and he took my tongue in his mouth.

So fucking hot.

I rubbed my cock along his, hard and hot, but I wanted more tonight. I wanted to be inside him. I wanted to come in him. I wanted to make him mine, over and over.

"Where's the lube?" I murmured, kissing down his jaw. "I wanna sink myself inside you so fucking bad."

He stilled, saying nothing until I stopped licking his neck and looked at him. "I didn't bring any. I thought you did."

"No, I thought you . . ."

He began to smile.

"Oh, thank God you're joking," I said.

He laughed. "I'm not. I didn't pack it."

I blinked. "Then why are you laughing?"

He put his hand to his forehead. "It is kind of funny."

I rolled my hips, letting him feel just how funny my dick thought it was. Then I had a thought. "I wonder if there's anything in the Esky we could use."

He wrapped his legs around me. "You're not using your mum's food as lube."

"Ugh, babe," I whined, falling onto my hand by his head. He was still hard and so was I, and this position wasn't doing us any favours. "You shouldn't wrap your legs around me like that."

He bit his bottom lip and brought my nose to his. "How good are you at maths?"

Huh?

"What?"

"Maths. How's your subtraction?"

"Normally pretty good, but right now I'm just confused. Please don't make me do maths. I'm not thinkin' with my big brain right now."

He smiled. "What's seventy minus one?"

Even my lust-addled and confused big brain could work that out.

I kissed him with smiling lips. "I'm gonna seventy minus one you so hard."

He laughed and unhooked his ankles behind me, so I manoeuvred myself on my side, my face in line with his erection in his threadbare shorts and his warm breath on my aching dick.

I slid my arm under his hip and pulled the front of his shorts down to free his gorgeous cock. I was so enraptured by this sight, by what we were about to do, that his warm, wet mouth took me by surprise.

"Oh fuck," I cried as he sucked me in.

And it would've been so easy to get lost in the pleasure, the heat and the glide, how he sucked . . .

I had to remember to focus on him.

So I took him all the way in, sucking and swirling my tongue, opening my throat. He moaned around my cock, his body trembling, and I didn't ease up. I worked him hard and fast, holding the backs of his thighs, his arse, as I swallowed around him.

He grunted, his body jerking in my arms, and his tongue worked its magic on me. So hot and wet, and he could suck so hard. I was close. I wanted to come so bad but I needed him to come first.

I snuck a finger in to draw a line along the seam of his balls to his hole. He bucked his hips, groaning around my cock, his entire body went rigid, and he shot his load down my throat.

His groan, his tightened throat, the way he held me

was enough to end me. My orgasm ripped through me and I tried to pull out, I tried to warn him, but he only held me tighter as I came.

He grunted with every spurt, with every wave of pleasure.

Until he finally released me and we both collapsed, breathing hard. My head was still spinning.

"You okay?" I asked.

"Mm. I think you broke my throat."

I barked out a laugh but sat up and helped him sit up too. I gently touched his throat. "Does that feel okay?"

He winced when he swallowed.

"Let me see. Open wide."

"No. Opening wide is what broke it."

I didn't mean to laugh, but given he was talking and joking, I was sure he was fine. "Okay, it's not broken. And just for the record, I tried to pull out and you pulled me in deeper."

He made a face and shrugged. "I'm not sorry in the slightest." But then he winced again when he swallowed.

"Let me get you a drink." I opened a bottle of water for him and he sipped it. "Better?"

He gave a nod. "I'm still not sorry."

I snorted. "Okay, but maybe rest it for a bit."

"Are you telling me to shut up?"

I chuckled. "No. Just take it easy. No singing."

"Have you ever heard me sing? Ever?"

"No."

"And for that, you can be thankful."

I leaned over and gave him a soft kiss. "I love you."

He gave me a smile and nodded, his cheeks red, immediately uncomfortable. "Same."

I knew he loved me. I did know that. But man, I had to admit, it started to hurt a little not hearing him say it. And it wasn't his fault . . . I knew that too.

So I tried to make a joke out of it and pretended he'd shot me in the heart. "Oh, so close, but yet, so far."

CHAPTER SEVEN
JEREMIAH

I'D NEVER EXPERIENCED INEPTITUDE. I'D NEVER FAILED AT anything. Well, social situations aside. I'd excelled at all academics. I'd excelled in my career. I'd excelled in any task I'd set my sights on.

But I felt as if I was failing Tully.

I was not a good boyfriend. I wasn't capable of reciprocating his affection declarations, and it was hurting him. He needed it, very clearly thrived on it, and I fell woefully short.

He tried to laugh it off, but I could see the hurt in his eyes.

He'd told me he loved me, as he had declared many times. And I'd replied with, "Same."

Same.

I hated that I was like this.

Before I could make things any worse, he stood up and held out his hand. "Come on, let's go outside and see."

He helped me to my feet. "See what?"

"See what we can see, see, see."

The way he sang it led me to believe it was a nursery rhyme. A child's song I'd never heard.

"Never mind," he mumbled.

Clearly, I'd failed at that too.

Outside, much like the direction my mood had taken, was getting dark. "Does this boat have lights?"

He nodded. "Yes. But we have an LED lantern. Better to use that than the battery on the boat."

He found the lantern and, opening the door, went out to the stern. There was still enough daylight to see, barely though. The skies were overcast and grey, clouds low, but no rain, and the water was dark. It wasn't as rough as before, but it wasn't calm by any means.

He turned the lantern on, holding it out and scanning the beach.

I was almost afraid to ask. "Any visitors?"

"Not that I can see. No eyes staring back at us anyway."

"It's not necessarily the ones you can see that bother me."

He turned and rubbed my back. "We're safe here. If you need to pee, go stand on the bow and aim with the wind, not into it."

"I'm not peeing off the front of the boat."

"Would you like to fill an empty water bottle again? You could give this one to the crocs too. We should absolutely patent Croc-ade. Pee-coloured electrolytes with crocodile teeth punctures on the label. Could be the new Red Bull."

I ignored that and didn't even bother rolling my eyes. "I'll be fine."

"If you gotta pee, you gotta pee. And if you should require a bathroom for any other reason, I suggest you do it now before we lose all light. There's a camping shovel, the kind that folds up, for you to go into the bushes and dig a hole."

I stared at him, and he tried to keep a straight face but failed. I gave him a playful shove. "You're not funny."

He laughed. "There's an enclosed head."

I squinted at him. "Is that a boating term I should be familiar with?"

Tully snorted. "Come on, I'll show you."

He revealed a hidden door and how there was, in fact, a full toilet on board. It was approximately the same size as the bathroom in my old apartment in Melbourne. "I don't want to know how much this boat cost, do I?"

He chuckled. "Probably not."

"Well, considering it's absurdly expensive—and you know I saw the radome on the roof—and now that we're not going to capsize, can we have a look at the weather radar system?"

He grinned at me, the soured mood from before seemingly forgotten. "Of course we can."

He showed me how to turn it on, and I was impressed with it too. Though, honestly, given my time in Darwin, I'd be impressed with any radar system that wasn't as old as I was. "This has a better system than my office."

"Well, that wouldn't be difficult, considering your office isn't operational right now. But they'll be starting soon, and it'll be state of the art. Everything."

"I hope so."

We watched the radar for a short time. There was a cloud band right across the screen. The rain had moved east and there didn't appear to be much left in the tail. He kissed my shoulder. "Feel better now that you can see it?"

I nodded. "Yes, thank you." I turned to him and pulled him closer. I might not be able to say some things out loud, but I could say this. "Thank you for before. You never ridicule me or make fun of me. And you know exactly how to make me feel better. I want you to know how much that means to me."

He smiled, not a full-wattage grin, not even really a happy smile. And I realised then the difference between his honest smiles—like the ones that made my heart skip a beat—and the one he wore now. They were so very different. "I know," he murmured. Then he put his finger to my lips. "You're supposed to be resting your throat."

So yes, I was failing at being a boyfriend.

I needed to do better. I needed to be better, try harder.

For him.

So I took his hand, turned it palm side up, and nervously drew a heart with my index finger.

Tully chewed on the inside of his lip before a smile broke out. A genuine smile this time. "Did you just draw a butt?"

I rolled my eyes and he laughed, pulling me in for a hug. He kissed my temple, and any hurt from before seemed to have dissipated. And that was Tully Larson—hurt for a brief moment before letting the sunshine-side of him win again.

My god, I didn't deserve him.

"It was a heart," I mumbled into his neck.

"It was a butt." Then he ran his hand to my arse and squeezed. "I happen to like butts."

I sighed, long and loud. "I'm tired. It's been a long day."

"Wanna call it a day?"

"I think so."

"Can I still hold your arse if we lay down?" He gave me another squeeze for good measure.

I snorted. "Fine."

When we lay down, I used Tully's arm as a pillow and sighed as tiredness crept over me. The gentle rocking of the boat was even kind of nice. "We're heading home tomorrow, yes?"

"Don't wanna stay for a few days?"

"I really don't."

Smiling, he kissed my temple. "We can try fixing that weather box stand in the morning, then head back with the change of tide in the afternoon. Sound okay?"

"Perfect. Thank you for bringing me out here. I don't mean to sound ungrateful, because I'm so thankful you're here with me. And I cannot believe head office thought I could come out here with anyone that wasn't you."

"Well," he said with a sigh, "even if someone else

brought you out here, I'd still be coming with ya." He rolled onto his side and pulled me into his arms properly. His eyes were closed. "No one gets you to themselves but me."

I smiled as I drifted off to sleep. "No one but you."

———

I woke up to an awful rocking, and for a not-fully-awake-moment, I'd thought I'd woken up drunk.

Drunk, I was not. I was still on this damn boat.

I was alone too.

"Tully?" I called out, getting up.

It was barely daylight, though still overcast, and the door was open. I walked out on somewhat unsteady feet, having to hold on to the wall. I couldn't see Tully anywhere. I tried not to panic. I couldn't see any crocodiles, but ugh, the water was rough; fast and uneven waves were rocking the boat. I went to the very back, about to step onto the rickety jetty. Panic started to rise in my chest. "Oh my god, Tully? Where are you?"

"Hey. I'm up here," he called out from the other end of the boat. Up on the bow, sitting with his feet over the edge like a madman. He was holding a fishing rod?

"Please don't dangle your feet near the water," I pleaded. "Crocodiles can jump, you know. Are you crazy? I thought you'd gone overboard and were missing, presumably taken by a crocodile, and you know I wouldn't know what to do."

He laughed.

Because of course he did.

"I was going to catch us a fish."

I looked around, trying to let my face show how displeased I was with that idea. "Oh good. Any bites?"

He laughed louder and began to reel his line in. "No bites. I thought with the overcast skies and choppy water I might have some luck."

He fixed his line and stood up, walking down the edge of the boat toward me, and I tried not to have heart failure watching him. He walked—barefoot, mind you—as if he were on solid ground and not a thin, narrow railing on a boat that was rocking in rough waters.

I held my hand out to him. "Please get down. You're scaring me."

He jumped down, grinning, and he took my hand to look at my watch. "Huh, elevated heart rate. Not my preferred method of raising your heart rate." Then his eyes met mine and he let out a disappointed sigh. "We forgot to wear the chest strap yesterday during our seventy-minus-one math lesson. We might need a repeat today . . ." Then he made a face. "Oh, how's your throat this morning?"

"My throat's fine."

"So we can have another math lesson? We both get gold stars at the same time."

I snorted. "I'm not opposed. As long as you fulfil the promise you made yesterday."

He squinted at me, confused. "What promise?"

"That you bury yourself in me when we get home and have lube."

His eyes widened, as did his smile. He palmed his dick. "Damn, babe. We could go home right now."

"We need to fix the weather box."

"Fuck the weather box."

I laughed. "It won't be the weather box that gets it, I can assure you. Should we have some breakfast? I'm starving."

He ditched his fishing rod and followed me inside. "No, I'd like to revisit the deep-dicking conversation. And the math lesson."

I found the container of orange segments, opened it, and held one slice up to Tully's lips. The boat was rocking so much that I almost missed his mouth. "Oh god, I'd really like to not be here anymore. On this boat, on this island." I had to hang onto the seat. "The sooner we try and fix the box, the sooner we can go, yes? You mentioned waiting for the tide. Do we have to do that?"

"No, it just means we'll have to navigate around sandbars. But that's okay." He held onto me by the arm. "You okay?"

I shook my head. "I'd very much like to go stand on some solid ground."

"Okay. Lemme just check the weather radar. It's still overcast out there, but the wind might determine if we have to leave now."

Splendid idea.

"Yes, yes. Sorry, I didn't think of that."

I didn't think of anything when I was stressed, apparently. Not in cyclones. Not on rocking boats. Tully thought clearly and rationally all the time, and all my mind could do was gather enough synapses for me to hold on to the seat while the boat rocked.

"Come and have a look," Tully said. "It'll make you feel better. Temp is twenty-four degrees. Humidity is at sixty-three."

He held his hand out for me and put his arm around me when I stood in front of the radar. A rain band covered the Top End, shades of blues and patches of greens meaning light to moderate rainfalls expected in the next hour or so. "Westerly wind speeds of ten to fifteen knots," I said. "Is that okay?" I knew what those numbers meant, but not what it meant to being on an actual boat in the middle of it.

"We need to leave by the time this comes in," Tully said, pointing to the deepening trough on the radar. "According to this, swells outside are at a metre already, and if we leave it too late, they'll be two metres, and you won't wanna be in that."

My stomach rolled. I didn't want to be in this now.

He squeezed my shoulder. "We need to be gone by ten, okay?"

I checked my watch. It was almost six thirty in the morning. Three and a half hours? "Easy."

He put on his boots, then took my wrist and looked at my watch. "Okay, before your watch overheats, we need to get you onto dry land."

"Are there crocodiles?"

He gave me a sad smile and shook his head. "Nope."

I was almost certain he was just saying that.

He put his hand to my chest, to see if he could actually feel my heart thumping; I was sure of it. "You okay?"

I nodded with more conviction than I felt. "Yes. Let's get this stupid weather box on its stupid stand so we can leave."

He helped me off the boat, then helped me along the jetty, all because my legs weren't connected to my brain, apparently. Even on dry land, it felt as if my knees would give way.

Tully held my elbow, trying not to laugh. "You good?"

"My legs have lost all structural integrity." My left knee wobbled right on cue and almost brought me undone.

He laughed as he helped me stay upright. "Walking helps. Come on, jelly legs."

We walked to the gate in the fence. Well, Tully walked; I wobbled like a newborn foal. And Tully put me straight to work.

He really was very good at distracting me. He knew exactly what I needed to get me out of my head. The frame the weather box stood on needed extra bracing, so he sent me in search of some branches or driftwood with strict instructions to not go too far.

He needn't have worried about that.

I wasn't keen on going too far at all. The very last thing I wanted to stumble upon was a crocodile nest in some shrub. There wasn't much in the way of vegetation to pick from, but Cyclone Hazer had made a mess, which made picking out some branches and twigs much easier.

I came back to the yard just as Tully was stomping a metal peg into the ground. All that was left of where the base had been fixed into the ground were two pegs, and he was adding a third.

"Found it by the fence," he said as he used the heel of his boot to stomp it down.

"Be careful," I urged. "Skewering your heel with a rusted metal spike would be extremely low on my idea of fun."

He laughed. "I got trusty boots. And no sledgehammer." He grunted with the last stomp and panted, his hands on his hips. "But if I can get the frame attached to the base, make it sturdier, and we are good to go."

I dumped my armful of sticks. "You're going above and beyond what is expected."

He picked up the first longer stick. "Well, they're gonna hafta come out and replace it anyway, but at least if we can get some kinda accurate reading, then comin' out here weren't for naught." He shrugged. "And if this stand falls over as soon as we leave, I don't give a fuck."

He set about bracing the frame with sticks and zip tying them together. It wasn't pretty, but it was a damn sight better than what I could ever put together.

And it worked.

We got the weather box placed on the frame, he fixed that with screws and zip ties, and after a good hour or so, it was done.

I went into the outhouse and checked the meters. "It's good!" I yelled.

Tully came in, all sweaty and concerned. "What's up?"

"You did it!" I said, giving him a kiss on the cheek. I was so proud of him. He did this. He fixed it all. It wasn't perfect and technicians would need to come out and get it all up to code. But he'd fixed it. This station would now be pinging accurate readings to the bureau.

The sky rumbled overhead. "Okay, that's our cue," Tully said. "I'll get the crate. You lock everything up. And let's go home. Where there is beer and lube."

I laughed. I wasn't looking forward to the trip home at all, but the beer and lube sounded like a great way to spend the afternoon.

After hot showers, of course.

We packed up the crate and I took some more photos before locking the outhouse door. Tully carried the crate and headed toward the boat while I pulled the gate closed. And just as I got the padlock through the bolt hole, I had a very strong, very sudden taste in my mouth.

Oh no.

I looked upward to the cloudy sky. Cumulonimbus clouds, low and darkening. It was drizzling rain, and thunder grated along the sky.

Something didn't feel right.

It didn't sound right, as if everything was in a vacuum. It made the hairs on the back of my neck tingle.

Oh god.

"Tully!" I yelled. "Get to the boat! Now!"

He turned as he was halfway to the jetty. "What was that?"

The copper suddenly filling my mouth was putrid. Far too strong, as if my mouth was filled with blood.

"Run!" I yelled, trying to get my body to move. To run, to sprint. To save him.

Then the sky went white, and everything went still before the silence exploded.

And then there was nothing.

CHAPTER EIGHT
TULLY

Jeremiah spun, the same way his mother had spun in that awful footage on Collins Street.

He danced the same way his mother had, his arm extended outward as he fell to the ground.

The deafening sound of the lightning, the blinding whiteness of it, was nothing when all I could see was Jeremiah being spun like that.

The void of sound as he crumpled to the dirt.

I hadn't even realised I was on the ground. The crate was knocked over. Had I been knocked off my feet?

I didn't remember falling.

I only saw him.

I clambered to my feet, scrambling to run back to him, sliding to where his body lay, his leg twisted underneath him. But his eyes . . .

So stark, so blue.

Open and staring.

"Jeremiah," I said, shaking him. "Jeremiah!"

Nothing.

No, no, no.

"No," I yelled. I shook him. I begged and touched his face.

Nothing.

So I banged my fists on his chest with all the strength that I had.

He sucked back a breath, as if he'd been rebooted, and he blinked.

Then he groaned.

I sobbed, fisting his shirt, my forehead on his chest. "Jeremiah, just breathe, baby. Just breathe for me."

He groaned again. The breath from his lungs sounded like an expiring tyre.

I stared at his face, making sure he could see me. "Baby, please. Stay with me, okay? You gotta stay with me."

He groaned again. His breaths were shallow, raspy. He tried to speak. Then he tried to sit up but couldn't. I shook my head. "Stay there," I said. "Don't move."

He needed help, and I had three choices: get him onto the boat and drive him back to Darwin myself, put out a radio call for help, or call for a medevac.

Medevac, Tully. Now.

I needed a phone.

Mine was on the boat where I'd left it yesterday. We had no service here because we were on a remote island in the middle of the fucking ocean, and I hated the bloody thing anyway. Jeremiah's phone was in his pocket because he'd been taking photos . . . I patted him until I found it and pulled it out . . . . it was hot. And completely dead. No, not dead. It was fried.

Fuck!

Wait. The satellite phone.

On the boat.

Dammit.

"Jeremiah, listen to me," I said. "Stay right here. Don't try and move. I'll be right back."

He groaned.

I didn't want to leave him, but I had no choice.

I sprinted for the jetty, not caring about which boards I trod on. I made it to the boat, ripped the door open, and found the phone in the console—seeing the emergency beacon and flipping it on—before racing back to Jeremiah.

He was now half sitting up, which probably was a good sign, but as soon as I slid in the dirt beside him, he fell back to the ground.

Christ.

I dialled 000, trying to stay calm.

"Police, ambulance, or fire," a woman's voice said.

"Police. Ambulance, coast guard. I don't know. Someone. I need a medevac—"

"Sir, what's your emergency?"

"My boyfriend just got struck by lightning," I said, tears burning in my eyes. "We're on Oxley Island at the weather station. He's breathing now, but he's in a lot of pain. He doesn't look too good." I sobbed. "Please send someone. Please hurry."

I DON'T EVEN KNOW WHAT HAPPENED IN THE MINUTES after. In the eternity after. I'd never been so happy to hear a helicopter in my life. I cried with relief at the sound. In fear too.

I'd never been so fucking scared.

Jeremiah was a little more aware. He was breathing okay but he still couldn't seem to speak, and he kept trying to sleep.

He was so damn weak.

By some miracle, the chopper landed up on the beach, and two medics ran over to us. They wore the green overalls and white helmets, just like you saw in the movies.

And they took him, just like you saw in the movies too.

I somehow had the cognizance to ask them where they were taking him.

Royal Darwin Hospital.

I was supposed to wait for the coast guard boat to arrive, but there was no way.

No fuckin' way.

The coast guard could arrest me or fine me or do what the fuck ever they had to do. But I wasn't waiting.

I collected the crate and threw it onboard, unmoored the boat, switched off the location beacon, and hit the engines.

I radioed the coast guard as I drove out toward Croker Island. I gave them the boat registration and told them my intended destination. I told them to call off the emergency, the vessel was fine, and I didn't need their help because I was fine.

I was not fine.

I was so very far from fine.

I steered the boat through the rain and rough swells with more speed and less caution than I probably should have for what felt like hours, and I had to keep remindin' myself to slow down because I'd be no use to Jeremiah if I capsized.

And I needed to see him.

As I came in south of Melville Island and as my phone beeped with a signal, I dialled my dad.

"Hey, Tull," he said.

As soon as I heard his voice, I burst into tears. "Dad, Jeremiah's been taken to the Royal hospital. I'm coming back now. I'm just at Melville Island. I'll bring the boat into the marina, but I'll need a car or a lift to the hospital."

I don't even know how I managed to speak or how he managed to understand me. But he was on it like I knew he would be.

I came into the main marina dock where he'd told me to go. There was no time for parking and mooring in our allocated bay. I didn't even shut the engine off. As soon as I got close, Dad stepped on board, I stepped off, and he took over. Mum put her arm around my shoulder and ran me to my waiting car.

"We'll be right behind you," she said, opening the passenger door for me.

Ellis was in the driver seat.

Like a military operation, my family had never let me down.

And I knew Ellis would have had a hundred questions, but he took one look at me and just nodded. "Christ. It's okay, Tull." He drove my car like he'd stolen it, and it still wasn't fast enough.

I wanted to tell him thank you. I wanted to tell him what had happened, but I didn't trust myself to speak.

"They choppered him in, yeah?" he asked.

I nodded.

"Then he's in the best hands."

I nodded again, wiping away a tear. "He better be okay. He just has to be."

Ellis slid his hand up my shoulder and squeezed the back of my neck. "He will be."

"Fuck, Ellis. He wasn't lookin' so good."

He gave me a gentle shake as we drove into the hospital grounds. "Hey. He'll be okay. But I tell ya what, I'll drop you off at the A&E and go and park the car. You need to tell them he's your husband, okay? Tell them you're married so they have to let you in to see him. They don't give a fuck otherwise."

I nodded, trying to pull myself together.

He pulled up at the emergency doors. "I won't be long. I'll find you."

I got out and went inside, heading straight for the triage window. The nurse took one look at my wet, dirty, tear-streaked face. "Can I help you?"

"Yes," I said. Then I remembered what Ellis had just said. "I'm here to see my husband. The medevac helicopter brought him in. He was struck by lightning."

Now, I don't know if it was what I said or how I could barely speak at all or if it was the look on my face, but she stood up and nodded toward the access door. "I'll buzz you through."

Ellis came running in at the right time, just as the security doors opened, and we went through, but the look on the nurse's face stopped me in my tracks . . .

Jesus, no.

"Is he . . . ? Where is he? Is he okay?" I couldn't quite catch my breath. "Is he . . . ?"

"This way," she said.

She still hadn't answered, and now my legs wouldn't work and Ellis had to all but make me walk. Through the corridors, the awful smell of hospitals, the fluorescent lights, the coldness of it all.

"I just need to know if he's okay," I said, trying to swallow back tears and the need to be sick.

The nurse stopped at what I now realised was the critical care ward. "Stay here, I'll get the doctor."

"Where is Jeremiah?" I asked, but she was gone. I went to follow. I needed to find him.

"Hey," Ellis tried, pulling on my arm. "We have to wait."

Why wouldn't anyone tell me where he was? "Jeremiah!" I yelled, heading toward the door. "Jeremiah!"

A doctor appeared with the nurse. A tall woman with a concerned scowl. "Excuse me," she said.

"I need to find Jeremiah Overton."

"Were you with him when he was struck by lightning?"

"Yes, I—"

"What can you tell me about it?" she pressed on. "Was it a direct strike? How close was—"

"Is he okay?" I asked, but my voice wouldn't work. "Is he alive?" I asked, louder this time. Ellis still had hold of my arm.

"Yes," she answered, and I almost went to my knees.

My god.

Thank God.

"Okay, let's sit you down," Ellis said, ushering me into a chair in the hall.

There was quiet talking around me. I heard my name over the blood pounding in my head, then the doctor leaned down to speak to me. "Mr Larson, my name is Doctor Jillick. Were you hit as well? How close to your husband were you at the time of the strike?"

I shook my head. "I don't know . . . maybe twenty metres. I think I fell down, but he . . . he spun. He was near the metal fence, and he spun and crumpled." I had to scrub at another tear. "Like a puppet when you cut the strings. He just . . . crumpled. And he was starin', and I don't think he was breathing. I don't know. I think I thumped his chest a few times and I just really need to see him. Please."

The doctor spoke to the nurse and the nurse disappeared, but then the doctor was shining her penlight in my eyes and holding my wrist—no, taking my pulse.

"I'm fine," I said. "I just really need to see Jeremiah."

"You said you fell down," the doctor said, still holding my wrist. Then the nurse was back with a machine, and she put a pulse thingy on my finger and an arm band on for blood pressure.

"Mr Larson?" Doctor Jillick repeated. "You fell down?"

"Uh, yeah, I was carryin' the crate of gear back to the boat, and then I wasn't. I was layin' in the dirt. I dropped the crate, I think. I dunno, I was too busy focusin' on Jeremiah to notice what happened to me."

"Okay, your pulse is a little above normal but regular. Your blood pressure is high—"

"Yeah, because I've had a bit of a rough day, not gonna lie."

"I'd like to get you checked out properly—"

"And I'd like to see Jeremiah," I said, standing up.

Ellis stood with me, holding my arm. "Tull, we need to make sure you're okay."

"I'm not okay," I cried. "I'm *far* from okay. I need to see him. Why won't they let me see him?"

And then I thought, *fuck it, I'll just find him myself.*

I sidestepped the doctor and went for the doorway opposite the nurse's station, but Ellis stopped me with his hold on my arm. I tried to break free, but then the doctor was in front of me.

"Mr Larson," she said sternly. "Don't make me call security."

"I just need to see him," I said. "For one minute. That's all. I just need to see him." I had to wipe tears off my face again. I tried to breathe but it came out as a sob. "If he's not okay . . ."

Ellis pulled me in for a hug and I fell into him, his strong arms holding me tight, holding me up, and he held me while I cried. "I just need to see him," I mumbled.

"I know."

He held me for a bit before he led me back to the

chair, and I was suddenly so freaking tired I could barely keep my eyes open.

Then Doctor Jillick came back. "Okay, you have one minute. You can see him for one minute. There were traces of heme pigments in his urine, so we've administered alkalisers to minimise renal complications. We're monitoring his heart, so don't be alarmed by the machinery. Lightning injuries tend to get worse in the few hours after before they get better."

I stood up, my heart in my throat, suddenly afraid to see him. To see how badly he was hurt. I couldn't get my legs to work.

"Mr Overton?" the doc said.

Ellis was beside me. "Come on," he said, urging me forward. "I'll go with you."

I swallowed hard and managed a nod. My feet felt heavy, my steps wooden. But I followed the doctor into the large room. There were a lot of cubicles, most with the curtains drawn, and the doctor walked to one in particular and stopped.

"One minute," she said, then pulled back the curtain. "He was very lucky. His ECG has shown some irregular function, his brain function is normal. We're running more tests and keeping him closely monitored."

She talked about entry points and exit points and the affected organs, but I couldn't quite grasp what she was sayin' because what I saw almost killed me. He was lying there, half a dozen machines beeping beside him, connecting wires to his torso. But he had a bandage wrapped around his head, covering his eyes.

His beautiful eyes.

"It's precautionary," the doctor said, and I realised that my hand was touching my own face, my eyes. "Eyes and ears are susceptible to damage in lightning strikes."

Yeah, of course.

"His pupils were dilating, and he was following movement. We don't believe he sustained retina damage."

I took his hand, but he didn't react. "Hey," I whispered. "It's me. I'm here. I'm right here."

Machines beeped and his lips cracked open. But his hand . . . his hand squeezed mine.

My knees almost gave out and I had to lean on the bed. I lifted his hand to my face and I sobbed. "You're gonna be okay," I said through my tears. "I'll be right here. You get some sleep. I'm not going anywhere."

Very slowly, he squeezed my fingers.

I'd never felt a more precious touch.

I leaned in and kissed his temple. "I love you," I whispered. The heart monitor beeped and I barked out a laugh. Then I kissed his bandaged eye. "Get some sleep, baby. I'll be right here."

The doctor walked me out and Ellis put me back in the chair. He fell into the seat beside me and rubbed my back. "Mum and Dad are on their way in," he mumbled, holding his phone. "I told them where we were."

I nodded, feeling better now that I'd seen him, but my god, I couldn't stop the tears.

"Mr Overton," Doctor Jillick said. "I'd still like you to get checked over."

I shook my head. "I'm fine, honestly, doc. I've just had a rough day." I scrubbed my hands over my face. "Thank you for letting me see him."

"No headaches?"

I shook my head.

"Difficulty breathing? Did you lose consciousness?"

"No."

"Blurred vision?"

"Only when I cry," I said, tryin' to be funny, but it didn't help that I was on the verge of more tears.

Ellis snorted, his hand on my knee.

The doc pursed her lips but gave a nod. "I would suggest perhaps going home for a few hours, but I—"

"I'm not leavin' him."

"I assumed you'd say that."

Just then, Mum and Dad pushed through the doors, Mum leading the charge. She stopped when she saw us, and god, it just started me crying all over again. I stood up and she collected me in a fierce hug.

"He's okay," Ellis said behind me. "Well, he will be."

"He's not out of the woods yet," Doctor Jillick corrected him. "He can expect to be here for forty-eight hours, minimum. He was very lucky."

"Oh, love," Mum said. She pulled back and cupped my face, only to drag me back in for another hug. "Of course he'll be okay."

The doctor cleared her throat, and Mum let go of me. "Can I suggest a visit to the cafeteria," the doc said.

"You can see him again in an hour or so. If there are any changes, I'll let you know."

"I told him I'd be right here," I said, but Ellis put his hand on my shoulder.

"She's asking us nicely to come back in a bit," he said. "So you don't have to leave the hospital, that's all. He's sleeping anyway, right?"

The doctor gave him a thankful nod and Mum thanked her, then led me out, her arm around my shoulder.

They sat me at a table in the cafeteria, Dad soon putting a coffee in front of each of us. I knew they'd need an explanation, so I tried to start at the beginning.

"He didn't even do anything crazy," I said. "He didn't run out in the storm. Hell, it wasn't even raining. It was just overcast, and we'd checked the radar beforehand. There was no lightning activity." I shrugged. "We were locking up the yard because he wanted to come home. Just about to get on the boat. And then he . . . he . . ."

Mum gave my hand a squeeze.

"He was putting the padlock on the gate, and I walked ahead with the crate with all his gear." I shook my head. "And he yelled something. I didn't understand what he said. But he was doing that thing with his mouth." I imitated the way he did it. "When he can taste it. Before lightning, he gets an awful taste in his mouth. Then he screamed at me to run, and there was a huge bang, like a bomb went off, and a flash . . ." My chin wobbled and I blinked back more tears. "Then I was on the ground. I think it knocked me over. I dunno.

But he was lying there." I couldn't stop the tears. I didn't even try. "The sight of him just lying there, all twisted, with his eyes open, staring, unseeing. I'll never forget it."

When I looked at my mum, she had tears rolling down her cheek.

"You did the right thing," Dad said gently. "You got him help."

I wiped my snotty nose with the back of my hand and Ellis handed me a serviette. I looked at my dad and nodded. "Sorry about just leaving the boat to you. I can go and clean it up later, I just—"

He shook his head. "It's fine, Tull. Don't you worry about anything."

"I activated the emergency beacon locator," I said. "I'll need to replace it."

He reached over and patted my hand that Mum still held. "You did the right thing."

I let out a shaky breath. "Thank you all, for coming to help. I don't know what I would've done."

"We're just glad you're okay," Mum said. "And we're glad Jeremiah is too."

"The doc wanted to check Tully out, but he refused," Ellis told them. "'Cause he got knocked over. Blowback or something like that, she called it."

"I'm fine," I added quickly.

"Tully," Mum started.

"I'm fine, honestly, I feel fine. Just worried about Jeremiah, that's all." I gave Ellis a look because he could have freakin' waited to tell them that. "I think he stopped breathing. When it happened. I dunno if it stopped his heart or if it was just shock, or what." I shrugged. "He was just staring, his mouth open. Maybe it was shock. I don't know. I pushed on his chest, I think. I dunno. It's all a blur."

Mum's tears started again. "But you got him here."

"And I was supposed to wait for the coast guard. The guys in the helicopter told me to wait for them. But I cancelled the request or I'd probably still be out there." I shrugged and looked at Dad. "You'll probably get a bill for that, so just give it to me."

"Don't worry about that," Dad said. "Drink some of your coffee. When did you eat last?"

I shrugged again and sipped my coffee. "I'm fine. I'm not hungry, to be honest."

Ellis disappeared and came back with a sandwich.

And then I got teary again, because I had such a wonderful family and Jeremiah was lying in that bed all alone. And I remembered something else.

"Oh god."

"What is it?" Mum asked.

I leaned my head right back and dug my thumb and finger into my eyes. How was I supposed to tell Jeremiah's father that what happened to his wife—the godawful horrible thing that ruined their lives—just happened to his son?

"Jeremiah's dad," I said. "I need to call him."

CHAPTER NINE
JEREMIAH

Everything hurt.

Everything.

My bones. My brain. My skin.

Everything.

I remembered Tully's face. Grey clouds behind him. A drizzle of rain. His wet hair. His tears.

His fear.

Then nothing.

Then there were lights and people staring down at me. A hospital. I remembered the doctors telling me to close my eyes, it would help, they said. They would cover my eyes because it would help, they said.

It sounded as if they were underwater.

Then everything was dark and the only thing that existed was pain.

Until that didn't exist anymore either.

But then there was a familiar touch. A hand in mine. A familiar voice. He sounded so sad. He was crying. But he was adamant and strong, and I clung to that.

He wasn't going anywhere.

He'd be right here.

Right here.

He wasn't leaving.

"Get some sleep," he said. "I'll be right here."

I clung to that with all I had left in me.

I woke up to more sounds. Beeping. Far-off voices. It sounded obscured but better than before. There was still only darkness, but someone had hold of my hand.

I didn't need to see to know who.

I squeezed his hand. I tried to speak, despite how dry my mouth was, how dry my throat was. "Hey."

"Jeremiah," he whispered. Tully's voice was like hearing heaven. "You're awake," he said. "Thank God."

I lifted my hands to my face, trying to find why I couldn't see.

His gentle fingers stopped me. "It's a bandage. The doctors said it was just precautionary." He squeezed both my hands and I felt the bed dip. His voice was much closer now, his breath warmer, and a soft kiss pressed to my forehead. "You're okay, baby. You're gonna be fine."

I sighed, resting, basking in the fact he was here. That he held my hands. That he loved me.

I tried to stay awake, to stay coherent, but the heaviness dragged me under again. Everything felt off-kilter. My heart, my breathing.

But I'd be okay. Tully said so.

And he still had a hold of my hand.

I woke up again to more voices. Quiet murmurs, familiar and warm. I knew he was close, but my hands were empty.

"Tully?"

"Oh, hey," he said, quickly taking my hand. "You're awake. You sound better."

A hand touched my other shoulder. So gentle. "Oh, Jeremiah, we've been so worried."

Mrs Larson.

She was here?

Tully snorted. "Mum's here. Dad and Ellis too, but they just went to get some drinks."

I still couldn't see, but my back hurt. Not like before. But as if I'd been lying down too long.

"Need to sit up," I said, trying to do exactly that.

I felt stiff and sore all over, and my head was woozy. My chest felt jittery.

"No, stay there," Tully said. "I'll go get the doctor."

He dropped my hand and Mrs Larson patted my other arm. "Oh, we're so glad you're okay. Tully's been out of his mind with worry," she said softly. "We made him go home and shower, at least, because he stank. But he came straight back."

"How long . . . ?"

"You were brought in this morning. It's now after six in the evening."

I tried to get my head around that.

"Do you remember anything?"

I tried . . .

"Just Tully."

Mrs Larson cry-laughed. "Of course." She patted my arm again. "You were brought in by medevac helicopter."

Helicopter?

I had flashes of being carried. Men with white helmets . . .

I shook my head.

I was dizzy and my heart felt fluttery.

Mrs Larson spoke quietly. "Tully called it in, then drove the boat back. I think he broke the speed barrier, but you're both okay and that's all that matters."

I wasn't sure what to say. Everything seemed so hazy.

"Oh," Mrs Larson said. "Before the doctor gets here, Tully told them you were married so they'd allow him to stay. Just so you know if the doctors or nurses refer to your husband."

My what?

"Husband?"

She patted my arm. "Shh."

"Oh, Mister Overton," a strange woman's voice said. "You're awake."

"It's doctor," Tully said. "Doctor Overton." A brief pause. "Oh, he's not a medical doctor. He's a genius doctor."

"Oh," the woman's voice said. "Doctor Overton. My name's Doctor Jillick. The medical kind."

I should hope so . . .

"Glad to have you with us," she said. "You gave us all a bit of a scare today."

"Need to sit up. My back hurts," I said. I tried for the bandage again. "Take this off."

An unfamiliar hand stopped me this time. Doctor Jillick, I assumed. "Okay, we'll sit you up first and I'll ask you some questions before we remove the bandages. How does that sound?"

"As if I have very little choice."

Tully snorted, though it sounded like he sobbed. "He's fine."

The bed began to incline, and I was soon half sitting up. I wasn't sure if it was better or worse. *Better, I think.*

"Can you tell me if you have pain?"

"Uh. Yes, though it's hard to localise. It's just . . . all over."

Tully took my hand again. The left, this time. Doctor Jillick was on my right.

Trying to garner some sense of space helped, and I tried to think about my body.

"My back. Lower back."

"It could be kidney related. We're running more blood and urine tests. You had some pigmentation present in your urine, which we've counteracted."

"Alkalisation."

There was a pause as if she was surprised I'd know this. "Yes."

"My head hurts," I said. "A dull headache. No sharp pain. I feel dizzy. My chest hurts—left side. My heart feels skittish. My right knee hurts. My teeth hurt. But I ache all over. My bones ache. Should a skeleton ache? I'm not sure it should."

Tully lifted my hand to his face. It seemed to hurt him to hear.

"Your brain activity is normal," Doctor Jillick said. "Your ECG is on the weaker side of normal and there is some atrial fibrillation, but that's not uncommon with lightning injury. We have you on medication for that, and we'll continue to monitor you for forty-eight hours. You have an electrical burn entry point on your left side near your ribs, which would explain the pain. You also have exit wounds on the soles of both feet," she said. "They're small, approximately five millimetres each, full-thickness burn."

Wow.

"A dull headache is expected," she continued, "and may not subside for a while, for weeks even. It's very common for headaches to persist after a lightning-strike injury. All things considered, you were very lucky."

A lightning strike.

I don't know why I was surprised to hear her say it.

There was a moment of silence. "Doctor Overton," she said, her tone different this time. "Do you remember being struck by lightning? You seemed surprised when I said that just now."

"I remember," I began, trying to recall. "I remember Tully's face . . . and seeing the sky. Nothing else."

He pressed my hand to his cheek. "You told me to run," he said.

I tried to remember more, but I had nothing.

"We were on the island," I murmured. "Then I was

here. I'd like to take this bandage off now." I pulled at the gauze again, and no one stopped me. I wanted to see what *here* looked like.

I needed to see Tully.

"Let me," Doctor Jillick said, and then she unwound the bandage from around my head. "Keep your eyes closed for me. And don't be alarmed if your vision's not normal. You may need to adjust."

I kept my eyes closed.

"The lights are low; things may appear dark. Open them, nice and slow," Doctor Jillick said.

I did as she said. My eyelids felt heavy and I realised now that, yes, my eyes hurt too.

I was in a bed, there were white curtains for walls. A woman with dark hair and a stethoscope stood by the bed, observing me, and Mrs Larson stood at my feet with tears in her eyes. But there, holding my hand, was Tully. He looked tired and hopeful.

Beautiful.

"Hey," I whispered.

He burst into tears and stood, pulling me in for an awkward hug, my face against his neck. His familiar scent and warmth made my head spin and my heart felt too full and jittery.

"Okay, he's had enough excitement for one day," Doctor Jillick said, urging Tully to pull back before she pressed buttons on one of the machines next to me. At least the beeping stopped.

Tully put his hand to my face and kissed me softly. He scanned my eyes, searching for something.

"Are they still blue?" I asked.

He grinned. "The bluest."

Then Ellis and Mr Larson came through the curtain, surprised but happy to see me. "Lightning McQueen," Ellis said. "You're awake."

Mr Larson elbowed him.

"Okay, this is far too many people," Doctor Jillick said, checking her watch. "You have two minutes, then everyone has to leave. Even husbands, sorry." She gave Tully a pointed nod. "This is the critical cardiac ward. Non-standard visiting hours apply."

"Even husbands, Tully," Ellis repeated with his usual grin.

Mrs Larson levelled him a look that shut him up. Even Mr Larson grimaced.

But something else . . .

"Cardiac ward?" I asked.

It was only then that I realised I had a chest full of sticky pads and wires.

Why was my brain so slow?

Doctor Jillick met my gaze, her stoic face giving nothing away. "Your heart stopped. You were wearing a heart monitor watch and a chest strap. We don't have the numbers from the chest strap, but those watches give us all kinds of information. Your heart rate went from eighty, to one hundred and forty, to zero. Hard to tell if it was the lightning strike that caused your watch to stop or your heart, but given the accounts by your husband and the point of entry at your ribs, it's likely." She looked at Tully then. "His soreness is a direct result of the electrical entry and the shock to his heart, not from any attempt at compression."

My heart stopped.

My heart.

Compressions?

I looked at Tully. "You . . . ?"

He nodded and half shrugged. "I wouldn't call it compressions. It was more that I punched your chest a few times because you weren't . . ." He shook his head, tears in his eyes. "I'm sorry if I hurt you."

Doctor Jillick shook her head. "I can assure you, Mr Larson, it wasn't you."

Tully nodded, and his chin wobbled. He didn't look convinced.

I put my hand to his face.

"You were very lucky your husband was with you," Doctor Jillick added.

I smiled at Tully, his face in my palm. "My husband."

"Okay, we'll get going," Mrs Larson said brightly. Changing the topic, probably. "Tully, Ellis will wait for you at the car. And Jeremiah, we'll be back in the morning. Get some rest, sweetheart."

I managed a smile and a nod as they left—Mr Larson led Ellis out before he could speak—and Doctor Jillick gave Tully a stern glare. "One minute."

Tully kissed my palm, and when we were alone, he met my eyes. "She says one minute a lot." He looked so tired, as if he'd had the worst day. "Jem, about the husband thing," he whispered.

"Your mum told me."

"Don't be mad or freak out," he added. "It's just quicker and easier."

I dropped my hand and patted the bed. "Can you sit up here?"

He sat on the edge of the bed. "You okay?"

I was so tired and short of breath. "Lie down with me."

He didn't need telling twice. He crammed himself on the edge of my bed, half lying on me, his head in the crook of my neck.

If I had one minute left with him, this was exactly how I wanted to spend it.

We didn't speak; anything that needed to be said could wait. We just lay there, his body, his warmth, all that I needed right then.

He made everything better.

Until Doctor Jillick pulled back the curtain, took one look at us, and sighed. She gave Tully a nod of her head that said it was time to leave.

He whined, but he got up. He kissed my forehead, then my lips. Right in front of her, and I didn't even care.

"Get some sleep. I'll be back at breakfast time."

Doctor Jillick said, "Visiting hours are—"

"I'll be back at breakfast time." He kissed the side of my head. "I love you." Then he paused for a second, staring into my eyes before pulling away. He gave me a nod with such sadness on his face, then disappeared behind the curtain.

Doctor Jillick talked about me trying a light dinner and how tomorrow, if my ECG continued to improve, I'd maybe get moved to another ward.

But I couldn't get the look on Tully's face out of my mind. Was he sad because he had to leave?

Probably.

But it looked like more than that.

"Doctor Overton?"

"I don't know if I'm terribly hungry," I said. The scent of the food being served to other patients was awful, and I was having trouble keeping my eyes open.

"Well, if you move to another ward, your husband can stay."

My husband.

My heart fluttered at the word, and I was suddenly utterly exhausted. "Then maybe I could try and eat something." My words sounded garbled, and I got butterflies in my chest, and I was very dizzy. I was having trouble keeping my head up.

"Jeremiah, look at me," Doctor Jillick said. She sounded mad. And far away.

I tried to focus, but the jitteriness in my chest stole my breath.

Then everything went dark.

CHAPTER TEN
TULLY

I ALMOST DIDN'T ANSWER THE PHONE.

Nobody answers unknown numbers, and for a moment I considered not answering it at all, but it was a local landline.

I'd been home for all of thirty minutes. I was in the kitchen and Ellis was insisting I eat somethin' before going to bed. It'd been one helluva day and I didn't really feel up to talkin' to anyone.

I half expected it to be a news reporter and I wasn't gonna answer it. Then I thought maybe tellin' someone to fuck off seemed like a good idea.

"Mr Larson," a voice said. "This is Doctor Jillick."

My knees buckled and the room tilted.

"I want to reassure you that your husband is stable, but we believe he's suffered a delayed ventricular arrhythmia episode. He's having a cardiac MRI—"

The room began to spin and I couldn't hear what else she said.

"Mr Larson?"

"I'm coming back," I said, looking for my keys.

"I would ask you not to, Mr Larson," she replied. "The ICU doesn't take visitors at this time. He's receiving the best possible care."

"That's great," I said flatly. "But I'm coming back. I'll sit in the hall if I have to."

I'd sit in the fucking car park for all I fucking cared.

I still couldn't find my keys.

I disconnected the call and was tryin' real hard not to lose my shit. "Where are my fucking keys?"

Ellis held them up, and for a split second I thought he was going to say no . . .

But he didn't. "I'll drive you."

I WASN'T JOKING WHEN I SAID I'D SIT IN THE HALLWAY.

I wasn't allowed in to see him, which wasn't a great surprise. I wasn't even mad. It took every ounce of control I had not to cry.

But in the hallway, I sat.

And that's where I was when my mum came in just after six in the morning. I must have dozed off because I startled when she sat down next to me.

"Oh, Tully," she whispered. "Ellis called us."

I nodded, trying to think clearly. I scrubbed my hand over my face. "I don't know how he is. I'm not allowed in to see him."

She rubbed my back. "He seemed okay when we left him yesterday," she whispered.

I nodded. "I know. Delayed symptoms, delayed

reactions. I dunno. It's common with lightning injuries." I shrugged. "The doc said he had a ventricular episode or something. Must have been right after I left. He was tired. I should have paid attention. I shouldn't have left."

"You didn't have a choice, love."

I blinked back tears, and my nose burned. "He needs to be okay."

She nodded, fighting her own tears. "He will be."

I sighed, my head falling into my hands. "He's studied lightning his whole life. And you know, it doesn't scare him at all. He'll run into a storm and lightning could rip the sky apart right over his head and he wouldn't even flinch. And he knows when lightning's gonna strike, Mum. He gets a funny taste in his mouth. It's a thing that happens to some people who've been struck . . ." I let out a teary laugh. "You know, on the island, he told me to run. Not himself. He has no self-preservation skills at all. I mean, at all. And after Cyclone Hazer when he saved those two kids, I made him promise me that he had to start thinkin' about me, and he couldn't just run out into a freakin' storm like that."

I shook my head, not even sure what or who I was getting mad at.

"He told me to run. So at least he was thinking of me, I guess."

Mum didn't say anything, just listened and let me vent. I wasn't making much sense, but god fucking dammit.

"I tell him I love him all the time," I said. "But he's

never once said it back to me. I make jokes about it and try not to let it bother me, but . . ." I shrugged. "I told him last night, before I left. I said, 'I love you,' and he . . . he said nothing."

"He wasn't very well last night," Mum said. "He was clearly not feeling well. I don't think that's anything to go by."

Maybe not.

But still . . . I couldn't stop thinking about it.

"He grew up so different to me. His whole life was . . . changed the day his mother died. And that's understandable. Anyone's life would be. I get that. But his mum died so publicly. He's reminded of it every other day, and it follows him everywhere, especially at his job. And you know if the media finds out that he was struck by lightning, my god, they'll have a field day."

"Then we don't let them find out. We protect him."

I nodded slowly.

She took my hand. "Do you think he doesn't love you?"

I couldn't stop the tears then, and I tried to wipe my cheek but it seemed pointless.

"I think he does. I joke about it because what else can I do? And I know he's not good with saying it. Talkin' about his feelings was never really allowed when he was growing up. He can't say stuff out loud, and I try to not let it bother me, but . . ." Fucking hell. "I guess it does."

"Oh, Tully," Mum whispered. "That man tells you

he loves you every time he looks at you. You're just not listening to his language."

I wasn't sure I followed. "What?"

"The way he looks at you," she said with a gentle smile. "He might not be able to say the words, but the way he looks at you . . . just screams how much he loves you. You need to listen in other ways. Listen to his love language, Tully. It's all right there. The way he looks at you when you're not looking at him. The way he smiles when you laugh. If you could see that . . . Tully, it's written all over his face."

I knew this.

I wasn't stupid, and I wasn't blind.

I saw the way he smiled at me, the way he looked at me. I could count all the little things he did for me, the way he looked after me. The way he touched me . . .

I sighed and scrubbed my hands over my face again. I was tired and stressed and scared.

"Ignore me," I mumbled. "I'm bein' stupid."

She patted my hand. "You're not stupid, love."

"It's not his fault. I don't blame him." I looked at her then. "It'd just be nice to hear it one time, ya know?"

She smiled sadly at me. "I know."

It took me a second to realise that someone was missing. "Where's Dad?"

"He had to go into the yard to check everything was done. The engineers are coming back tomorrow, and you know he's been waiting. He'll be here when he can."

Oh, work. I hadn't given work a thought. "Yeah. Fair enough."

"When does Jeremiah's father get here?"

"Tomorrow afternoon at three o'clock. He doesn't know yet. Jeremiah doesn't know. I didn't tell him yet."

"I'm sure he'll be grateful. They both will be."

I wasn't sure about that.

"I really want to see him, Mum. When can I get in to see him?"

She checked her watch. "It's almost seven."

The double doors opened and I was surprised to see who walked in. Rowan and Zoe. They stopped when they saw me, their eyes going to Mum.

"Is he . . . ?" Rowan asked.

"We haven't been allowed in yet," Mum answered. "All we know is that he's stable." She gave my knee a shake. "And that he's in good hands."

I must have looked like a wreck because Rowan walked over to me, pulled me to my feet, and hugged me. Strong and warm, he patted my back. Then Zoe gave me a quick hug too.

It just made me all teary again.

"Ellis called us," she said, her eyes full of concern.

I nodded just as a doctor came out. I hadn't seen him before. "Mr Larson?"

I turned, my stomach in knots, my heart banging to the point of pain. "Yes."

He smiled, taking in all the expectant faces staring at him. "Am I talking to everyone, or . . . ?"

"Yes, please." I doubted I'd hear or understand any of it.

He gave a nod as though he assumed as much. "Last

night, his ECG revealed an irregular wide complex tachycardia with a variable—"

"In English, doc," I said. "Please."

He smiled again. "Last night, his heartbeat became so fast and irregular it caused him to lose consciousness. A delayed electrical shock reaction, more than likely. He was treated with defibrillation."

Oh my fucking god.

"You had to shock him back to life?"

I suddenly felt faint. Or like vomiting.

My mum tightened her hold on me.

The doctor gave a nod. "He was lucky the doctor was with him when it happened. His heart rate is now back in the normal range, though he's weak and we can expect him to be tired and lethargic for some time."

"But he'll be okay," I tried again.

"His heart has sustained some muscle damage," he said. "His recovery will be slow, and I'm hesitant to say he'll make a full recovery, because the truth is the full extent of lightning injuries aren't often known for weeks or, in some cases, years."

"What do you mean muscle damage?" I asked. "The whole heart is muscle, so what does that even mean?"

"The MRI also showed signs of takotsubo cardiomy-opathy. More than likely brought on by the tachycardia and the defibrillation. That's not unheard of."

Tako . . . cardiomyopathy.

I'd heard of the cardio part, but I didn't know what it meant.

"Is that . . . takesumo-something. What is that?"

"It's a heart condition, brought on by an extremely

sudden stress, where the heart's lower left ventricle changes shape and enlarges." He shook his head. "Honestly, we can't say exactly what brought this on. Could have even been from the tachycardia episode on top of the thirty million volts he took in the lightning strike. From the markings on his chest, it looks like it hit him on the left side of the ribs, directly near the heart. He's very lucky to be alive at all."

"Sorry, doc," I said, still trying to get my head around any of what he'd just said. "Is it bad? The tako . . . thing? That's different to the tachycardia?" I was so confused.

He gave a nod. "Yes. Two different conditions. The tachycardia—the irregular heartbeat—has been corrected, for now. Takotsubo cardiomyopathy, the enlarged ventricle, is a temporary condition and should heal in a few months. It's not likely he'll require surgery. He's been administered medication, but with a healthy lifestyle and proper rest, it is completely manageable."

"That's good, yes?" I asked.

The doctor gave a nod. "All things considered, yes." He looked at us all in turn, his gaze returning to me. "His heart rate is regular, but—"

But it was good last night too, I thought.

"He's very weak and tired. He'll need complete rest."

"And his recovery?" Mum asked. "Do we need a recovery plan? What do we do now?"

The doctor paused, his gaze meeting Mum's with a smile. Like he appreciated that one of us was keeping up. "There will be a recovery plan, yes. As for the full recovery . . . We can't answer that definitively. People who survive lightning injuries may suffer side effects for weeks or even years afterwards. Some never fully recover."

"I know. He knows," I added. "It's not the first time he's been hit."

The doctor stared at me.

Shit.

"He was two years old. It wasn't recent. He . . . he studies lightning. He's a fulminologist. A meteorologist. He's a doctor . . ." I felt every second of the sleep I'd missed. "Can I see him? Please? I just really need to see him."

He had a nurse lead me through the very quiet, very horrible ICU. The doctor stayed back to talk to my family, no doubt asking all about what I'd just said. And they could tell him everything—about Jeremiah's mother, about him being the meteorologist who saved lives during Cyclone Hazer, about him going viral for almost getting struck by lightning when he saved Casey and Presley, about any of it—I didn't care.

I just needed to see him.

He was lying back at a slight incline, his eyes closed. There were more machines now. But the blankets were only up to his waist, shirtless with white monitor pads stuck all over his chest.

But holy shit . . .

His chest and up his neck were covered in a red vein-like pattern that I'd read about but never seen. It looked like lightning but on his skin.

Lichtenburg figures.

Spreading out from his left side, they crawled outward, like macabre capillaries. Like lightning had painted itself on his skin.

It was a phenomenon common in lightning injuries, and I knew they weren't painful, but they were very confronting proof that the lightning had touched him. What it had done to his circulatory system. What it had done to his heart.

Proof of how close he'd come to dying.

I took his hand, and he slowly opened his eyes. He saw me, slow-blinked, and his lips pulled upward in a smile. "Hey."

My nose burned and my eyes welled with tears. "Hey. You gotta stop tryin' to die on me, okay?"

He smiled a little more. "Okay."

"How are you feeling?"

"Better now. Heart not so jittery," he said. "Good drugs."

I laughed despite my tears. He did seem a little drowsy. "We need to look after your heart, you hear?"

He slow-blinked again, his gaze fixed on mine. "Yeah."

"You've got some pretty cool Lichtenburg figures all over your chest."

"I do?"

I took my phone out and snapped some quick photos, then held the screen up so he could see them.

"Well, shit," he said.

I laughed because it wasn't like him to swear. I kissed the side of his head. "You're gonna have a whole lot of data to study after this. They ran bloods and brain scans and all kinds of tests."

He didn't reply to that, and when I studied his face a little, his eyes were trained on mine. Almost like he was seeing me for the first time.

"You okay, babe?" I asked.

He smiled again, slow and dazed. "I love you," he murmured.

My heart thumped and my pulse rapid-fired in my veins. *He just said . . . He just said the words. He just told me he loved me.*

He was high, mind you. On whatever drugs they'd given him. But he'd said those three words I'd been dyin' to hear.

I barked out a laugh and wiped a tear from my cheek. "I love you too."

He slowly lifted his hand to my face, his eyes scanning me like he was tryin' to commit it to memory. "It's true. Always been true."

I nodded, holding his palm to my cheek. "I know. But thank you for saying it."

"Should have said it before now." He was getting tired again, his blinks getting longer. "Not afraid anymore. Need you to know it."

I cried into his hand, nodding, and I kissed his palm. "I know, Jem. I know. But I gotta say, it's real nice to hear it."

He smiled and closed his eyes. "So tired."

"Go to sleep, baby." I kissed his forehead. "I'll be right here."

"Right here," he mumbled.

I brushed his hair from his forehead as he slept, taking in his beautiful face.

I didn't even notice the doctor was standing at the foot of the bed. He kinda startled me. "He's asleep," I said, like he couldn't see that himself.

"He'll be very tired for a while," he said.

"But he'll be okay, right?"

The doctor's expression gave nothing away. "He's young and very healthy. He shouldn't have survived at all. The fact he's made it this far . . . his odds are good. Other concerns may present themselves, but for now, he's stable. Maybe you should get yourself some break-fast. The nurses tell me you've been in the hallway all night."

"I can come straight back though, right?"

He gave a nod. Even smiled. "Sure."

I followed the doctor back out to the hall where my entire family stood. Dad and Ellis were there now too. All their eyes zeroed in on me, waiting for some kind of news.

"I spoke to him. He said he feels better and that the drugs were good, and he swore," I said with a teary smile. I tried to get a hold of myself, but seeing the concern on their faces, all I had was more tears. "God, I'd really like to stop fucking crying."

Mum gave me a hug, and then Ellis joined us, and he fake-whispered, "What kind of drugs?" I nudged him, but I knew he was joking. "Come on," Ellis said, his arm around my shoulder. "You need food. Did you sleep at all?"

"Don't think so."

"Then we'll all have breakfast," he said. "Like the freaking Brady Bunch."

And we did. All six of us.

I couldn't remember the last time the six of us had sat around a table and eaten breakfast together. Not since I was a kid.

But it was real nice.

My siblings and I didn't always agree, but all our differences aside, I knew they loved me. And Jeremiah. They loved him too.

It bolstered me, gave me strength to get through the next few days. I knew they'd be tough. Tougher for Jeremiah still.

I managed to eat something and I choked down a terrible cafeteria coffee, but I needed to get back to him. Everyone hugged me and they waited until I was the one to walk away.

And holy hell, walking back into that awful ICU was frightening.

All those machines and the terrible smell of sickness and mortality . . . I was glad when Jeremiah's nurse pulled the curtain around, blocking it all out.

Just me and him.

I sat beside his bed and took his hand.

His eyes were closed, he looked peaceful. The wires and sticky pads stuck all over his chest were a reminder that his peacefulness was chemically induced. The morbid patterns on his pale skin were fascinating and beautiful and terrible.

His thumb stroked my finger, and I looked up to find him watching me.

"Are you perving on me?" I asked.

He smiled. "Yes."

"Just as well." I stood up and kissed his forehead. "I missed you."

He huffed out a quiet laugh. "Missed you too."

I sat back down, his hand in both of mine. "My family all said to say hi and that they love you, and they want you to rest and get better."

He stared at me.

"All of them," I added. "They were all here. Even Rowan and Zoe. They came for you."

He gave a slight shake of his head. "They came for you."

"They came for you, Jem. Mum's been here almost as much as me. Dad had some stuff to take care of at work but he came straight back. Ellis has been doing the rounds, keeping everyone up to date, and he's been an absolute rock. Well, as much as a nut sac can be an absolute rock."

Jeremiah snorted quietly.

"They love you," I said. "Like I love you."

His fingers squeezed mine. "Like I love you," he whispered.

I met his gaze, and he met mine right back. No looking away, no blushing, no eye-rolling.

"I don't know why I was so scared to say it," he murmured. "I thought it was foolish and unnecessary. I was wrong."

I kissed his knuckles, then I stood up and kissed his cheek, his eyebrow, his nose, his lips.

"I should have told you every day," he whispered.

"You can. Starting today. I'll make up another chart and we can add gold stars for every time you say it."

He smiled for a moment; then it faded. His eyes filled with sadness and regret. "I thought I was going to die," he whispered. "And you being here kept me here, I'm sure of it. Kept me tethered here. Knowing you were here. Knowing you loved me." He shook his head, his eyes full of tears. "I had to tell you. You needed to hear it, and I'm sorry I was a fool before."

I swallowed back my tears. "I'm trying to not cry anymore today, and you're not helping." I sat on his bed and tried to give him a hug, but it was awkward, so I lay my head on his chest instead. "I want to hear your heart," I mumbled. "I want to hear it strong and forever."

His hand found my hair, and his blinks were already getting slower.

"You almost did die," I said. "Twice. They had to use the paddles on you, like they do in the movies."

His fingers stopped in my hair. "I don't remember . . ."

"Probably just as well." I listened to the *thump th-thump* of his heart, the most precious sound. "I'm glad I didn't see it. I don't think I'd have survived."

"I'm sorry," he whispered, a tear rolling down to his temple.

I wiped it away. "But you're okay now. The doc said your heartbeat's back to normal and we just need to watch it and be careful, and you'll probably need medication for a while, and if that's what we have to do forever, then so be it."

He nodded.

"And I was thinking that we can get you a new watch and somehow sync it to my phone as well, so I get your heart-rate alerts too. I dunno if someone's invented that yet. Or maybe you can wear a chest strap every day and I'll get the readings on my phone. That might be better."

He chuckled softly. "Sounds good."

I sighed, putting my head on his chest again, listening. "I can see straight up your nose."

He laughed then, and I sat up, taking his hand again. "I missed your smile," I murmured. "And your eyes. And everything about you. I was really scared, and I'm thankful more than words can say that you're still here."

"Me too." His eyelids half closed. "I'm tired, Tully. I'm so tired."

I put my hand to his cheek and gave him the best smile I could manage. "The doc said you would be, and that it's normal, and that you should rest and sleep a lot. So don't fight it. I'll be right here. All day. Until they kick me out."

He smiled as his eyes closed. "Right here," he mumbled as he fell asleep.

So I sat there, watching him sleep, watching the machines like I had any clue what any of them did. But I watched those little heart lines as if they meant the world to me.

Because they did.

They were steady and consistent, pulsing the sweetest beeping sound in the world.

I watched them, and I watched him.

Until an hour or so later when his eyes opened again, and he smiled. "Still right here," he said.

"Just like I promised." He was thirsty, so I got him a drink of water and helped him sip it through the straw. He seemed a little brighter, so I took his hand and kissed his knuckles. "I forgot to tell you something."

"Oh, what's that? That you love me, or that you can see up my nose?"

I chuckled. "Well, both of those still apply, obviously. But I called your dad."

He seemed surprised by this. "You did?"

"Of course. And he's coming to see you. He'll be here tomorrow."

CHAPTER ELEVEN
JEREMIAH

My father was coming.

My father was coming here to see me.

Tully had called him, which I understood. But he'd also insisted my father fly into Darwin as soon as possible. Tully had arranged and paid for the ticket without hesitation. I didn't like the fact he'd paid for it, but it was very much a Tully thing to do.

We both knew there was no way my dad could afford it on his own, and he'd have to take days off work, which he never liked to do.

Yet, he'd agreed to come.

Perhaps because Tully had asked him and not me.

Not that I had ever asked him. I didn't want to inconvenience him . . .

I tried not to think about it.

He wouldn't arrive until later tomorrow afternoon, so I had a good twenty-four hours to get used to the idea. Twenty-four hours to rest and regain some strength.

I felt so weak and tired. It was disconcerting how just lying in bed and breathing could be tiring.

The doctors came and went, telling me everything that had happened and that would need to happen in the next forty-eight hours. I'd be hooked up to these machines for two days, then maybe I could move to another ward.

Tully sat by my side, listening and nodding. He held my hand and smiled at me, a beacon of reassurance in an otherwise dark and frightful time.

And I *was* scared.

Scared what this meant—for me, for him, for us. For my work, for everything.

Yet Tully never baulked, never faltered, never flinched.

He'd said he'd been scared enough the first day, he'd cried a river of tears. Now he was all positivity and sunshine.

He sat on my bed and fed me small triangles of sandwiches. He said they were 'coronary friendly,' and his nose scrunched up as though tomato and cucumber on wholemeal sounded atrocious, but they were the sweetest, most delicious thing I'd ever eaten.

They did kick him out for a few hours, but I slept the whole time he was gone, only waking up when he came back in. He was with Ellis this time, and Ellis took one look at me and stopped.

"Holy shit, that's so cool," Ellis whispered. He was staring at my chest, and I moved to pull the sheet up. "Sorry, dude, but have you seen yourself?"

"Leave him alone," Tully said, fixing my sheet for me. "Yes, I've shown him."

Ellis ignored him, took his phone out and reversed the camera so I could see myself. My chest. The Lichtenburg figures. The red lightning mapping out the veins and arteries under the skin.

"Does it hurt?" he asked.

I shook my head. "No."

I tried to sit up and Tully helped with the bed. It made it easier for me to look down at myself. The marks were concentrated on my left side, sprawling out like red lightning across my torso and neck.

"Always thought these were cool too," Tully said. "Until I saw them on you." He shuddered. "I don't like the reminder. Maybe I'll look back at some photos in a few years and think it was cool, but not now."

I looked up at him. I'd have thought he would have loved seeing them—they were a rare phenomenon, after all—but he really didn't. I reached for his hand. "They'll fade. Apparently."

"Well, I think they're cool," Ellis said. I think he'd taken some photos. "You look like one of those hotted-up cars with the flames up the side."

I snorted, but Tully grumbled and ignored him. He kissed the side of my head. "Did you sleep okay?"

"Mm."

"The nurse said you're doing well."

"If sleeping can be considered an accomplishment."

Ellis snorted out a laugh, then remembered to keep the noise down. "I better get going. Mum said she'll be around this arvo to see ya." He gently patted my leg.

"Good to see ya doing well, Jem. You got a bit of colour now." And then he leaned in and whispered, "And don't listen to him. The mean-machine flames are fucking cool."

Tully looked for something to throw at his brother. I could see that he considered the drinking cup from the tray, and I think Ellis saw too, because he grinned and waved as he disappeared out the curtain.

I smiled at Tully. "At least he didn't call me Lightning McQueen."

He rolled his eyes and sighed. "Yeah look, about that. I think he ordered balloons to be delivered. He tried for flowers but they're not allowed in this ward. Something to do with pollen and allergies and incredibly ill people. So anyway, he ordered balloons, and from the stupid grin on his stupid face when he told me, I think we can assume it's either Lightning McQueen related. Or pornographic. It really could go either way."

I chuckled, and he cupped my face and kissed my lips.

"Ugh, my breath must be terrible," I mumbled.

He clearly didn't care. "So I was doing some research on diets for a healthy heart, and it looks like we'll be eating a lot of grilled fish and salads. Which is fine by me. But I also thought about exercises we could do, and I know you used to swim when you were in Melbourne."

"Well, yes, but—"

"Because people can't talk to you while you're doing laps. I know. I remember. But I was thinking we could install a lap pool at home, on the strip that fronts the ocean."

"No."

"As long as we make it crocodile proof—"

"No."

"But then you could do laps for exercise and I could watch you, because I like it when you're wet, not gonna lie."

"Tully, you're not putting a pool in for me."

"It would be for me as well."

My nurse peeked around the curtain. "Oh, good," I said. "Can you please tell him that putting in a pool for me to exercise in, while being a lovely gesture and all, is a ridiculous waste of money?"

She looked at him. "I don't care about the pool, but you come in here and argue with my patient and I'll give you a lovely gesture of my own."

Tully pouted like a four-year-old, and I smiled. "I win."

The nurse came in, checked the machines, checked my IV bag, and put her hand on my arm. "Everything okay? Does your husband need to go?"

I smiled at Tully. "No, he can stay."

Tully was still pouting. "I'll be good."

She gave a nod and left us alone, and Tully sat in his chair. "The pool conversation can wait until we get home."

I sighed and held out my hand for him to take. He slid his fingers through mine and I tightened my hold on his hand. "I love you," I whispered.

He perked up, his pout now that smile that won me

over from day one. "I'll never get used to you saying it. I think you're gonna need to say it every day just to be sure."

"Okay."

He kissed the back of my hand. "You're tired again. You should close your eyes. I'll be right here."

I was tired, that was true. "Yeah. But I'm hungry," I said.

Tully stood up. "Then I'll get you something. You name it."

I pointed to my lips.

He grinned and leaned in, kissing me.

"And another sandwich would be great."

He kissed my forehead. "Your wish, my command."

He disappeared out the curtain and I must have dozed off again, because when I opened my eyes, he was sitting beside my bed, his arms crossed, his chin on his chest, sound asleep.

There was a cucumber and tomato sandwich on my tray table and a small apple juice.

And a huge bunch of balloons on my side table.

Lightning McQueen, of course.

After eating and taking another nap, I felt so much better. I was getting stronger and able to stay awake longer as the day progressed.

Mr and Mrs Larson called in to say hello, and after Tully fed me dinner, they took him home. And when I say he fed me dinner, I mean that he sat on the side of the bed and spoon fed me dinner.

I wasn't even embarrassed or annoyed.

It just made me happy.

And playing the charade of husbands didn't bother me at all.

In fact, I was getting used to it.

Liked it, even.

Perhaps it was cliché, but almost dying made me realise what was important. I didn't want to waste any more time.

More to the point, I didn't want to cut my time short. Not that I ever did so deliberately, but there had been times when I'd been reckless or blasé.

Those days were over.

I wasn't sure what it meant for my career. I would always be a meteorologist. I loved what I did. I loved my work at the bureau, and I loved the magnificence of Mother Nature.

But as for my personal quest to study the effects of lightning on the human body . . .

Well, I think I'd learned all I needed to know.

I'd been incredibly lucky to survive at all. Tully had been there to save me, and yet my brush with lightning, my very nearly dying because of it, had almost killed him too.

Not physically. It hadn't stopped his heart as it did mine, but I'd broken his. I'd put him through hell.

And if he wanted to sit on the side of my bed and feed me gentle spoonfuls of food, then I would never object.

The installation of a pool was still a hard no, though.

I had to draw a line somewhere.

"Someone looks a little brighter tonight?" the doctor said. He came in, smiling, checking my charts on his iPad.

"Feel much better."

"Heart rate's good," he said. "No light-headedness or pain?"

I shook my head. "No."

"Good."

"How long will I be in this ward for?"

"We'll take another ultrasound of your heart tomorrow, then we'll see about maybe moving you back to the cardio ward, depending on what we find. How does that sound?"

"Good."

"One step closer to going home, huh?"

I nodded.

Home. Wherever Tully was, was home to me.

"I'd really like that."

"I spoke to your partner about home care."

"Husband," I corrected automatically. It was a lie, but it gave me a thrill to say it.

I'm surprised the ECG didn't beep.

"Sorry, husband," the doctor said sheepishly. "He said twenty-four-hour home care is an option."

Of course he did.

"If it gets you home quicker," he added.

That made me smile.

"I explained it would require an ECG machine similar to this one and he had no objections."

I tried not to smile so big. "Of course he didn't."

He nodded slowly, checking the chart again. "I asked him why you were wearing an athlete's chest strap monitor."

Oh no.

"Uh."

He chewed on the inside of his lip. "First, he blushed and his brother laughed. So I could only assume . . ." He smirked at me. "Then he explained that you monitor your heart rate during electrical storms and that you've had a few close calls with lightning before."

I inhaled deeply and let it out with a sigh. "I did, yes. But I think those days are over."

"He said you chase storms together."

"He's a storm chaser. I'm a meteorologist."

He nodded. "Yes, who issued the warning alert for the cyclone. Created quite the hype if I recall."

At least he didn't mention my mother, though if he knew who I was from Cyclone Hazer, it was like he knew anyway . . .

"And saved two children from a lightning strike," he added.

"Yes, well, I think I'll be staying indoors from now on," I said. "My fulminology days are over. If I were a cat, I'd be on my ninth life." I inhaled deeply, realisation that my studies were over really sinking in. "After my last close call, Tully told me I needed to consider him instead of almost dying to save other people. I think I'll do just that."

He nodded slowly. "Well, as a doctor, I'm inclined to

agree with him. No more lightning strikes. I can almost guarantee the next one won't be so kind."

I considered telling him I hadn't deliberately endangered myself in the name of science. Not this time, anyway. But what was the point? It didn't make any difference now.

In the end, all I could do was sigh.

He checked my burns, my small exit wounds on the soles of my feet. According to the doctor, they looked like cigarette burns. As if someone had extinguished cigarettes on my skin. The one on my ribs was much the same.

Fascinating that the entry and exit of so many volts could be so concentrated, so small.

The Lichtenburg figures were beginning to fade from my neck, though were still darker at my ribs.

My ribs hurt the most now, which was probably a good sign that the rest of me had stopped hurting, that the pain was mostly gone. My heart and chest were still tender, and it helped to keep my breaths measured.

But the doctor was happy with my progress.

"Get some sleep," he said. Then before he turned to leave, he nodded at the balloons. "Someone has a sense of humour."

I smiled. "Yes, he does."

Sleep didn't come easy, as tired as I was. I could doze off well enough, though my mind kept returning to my earlier realisation.

My fulminology days were over.

I still had my job, of course. And I would always

love meteorology. But I couldn't risk another strike injury.

Not that I'd risked myself this time. And maybe that was what annoyed me the most. I hadn't run out into a clearing in the midst of electrical activity. I hadn't wrapped myself in foil, as Tully had once suggested, to go and stand out in a storm with a death wish.

I'd simply been in the wrong place at the wrong time.

Like my mother had been.

I wasn't sure what it meant for me and Tully.

He loved storm chasing. He'd lost previous relationships because of his commitment to it. He'd spent weekends and every holiday out in the wilderness to simply be in any storm he could find.

And he'd said that he couldn't believe how lucky he was to have someone he could share that with.

But what if he could no longer share that with me?

Sometime in the middle of the night, my nurse came in with a frown. She checked my machines. "Everything okay?" she asked. "Your heart's a little fast; blood pressure's on the rise."

"I'm okay," I said. "Just thinking."

"Thinking or worrying?"

I snorted.

"All you're doing is adding stress on your heart. So how about we try and sleep instead?"

"Hm."

She gave me a smile. "No worrying allowed. Or I'll tell that gorgeous husband of yours."

That made me smile. *Husband.* "No tattletales, please."

Happy with the machines and whatever output I was now showing, she patted my arm. "Get some sleep. You've got a big day tomorrow."

An ultrasound, with hopefully good findings. Maybe moving to another ward.

And my father's arrival.

A big day indeed.

———

TULLY'S BRIGHT AND SMILING FACE GREETED ME AFTER breakfast. He planted a kiss on my forehead, then my cheek. "What did they make you eat?"

"Cold toast and black tea."

He made a face. "Christ."

"There was a porridge-like substance but—" I shook my head. "I stopped eating craft glue when I was in preschool."

Tully laughed, his brown eyes shining.

"Wow," he said. "You were ahead of the class. I didn't stop eating craft glue until year three, at least."

I'd do anything to keep him smiling like that.

"I was a gifted child."

"Can I get you anything from the cafeteria? From an actual café? A proper coffee?"

"Maybe later." I took his hand, just wanting to hold it.

He perched his backside on my bed and played with

my fingers. "You okay? The nurse said you didn't sleep too well."

"She's a dibber dobber."

"Jem?"

I sighed. "I just spent a lot of time thinking. I can't do much else."

The hold on my hand got a little tighter. "Thinking about what?"

"About what I do now."

"What do you mean?" He was worried, a little pale even. "Are you talking about us?"

Oh god. He thought . . .

"No, not like that. Not about us."

He sagged, visibly relieved. "Christ, Jem. I was about ready to call for the crash cart. You almost gave me a heart attack."

"Well, you're on the right ward."

"True." He put my hand against his chest. "Feel that?"

I could feel the thrum of his heart under my palm. I smiled, then nodded to the ECG machine. "Mine comes with pictures."

He smiled but his eyes scanned mine. "What were you thinking about? You're still kinda scarin' me, not gonna lie."

"Well, I . . ." I wasn't sure how to say this, and I could only guess honesty was the best policy. "I'm not sure I can continue with my fulminology studies."

He seemed confused by this.

"Okay." He squinted at me. "I'm not sure what

you're saying. Are you talking about your work at the bureau?"

"I'm not sure," I said. "I'd like to stay. I love my job, and if they ever get around to upgrading my office . . ." I looked at our joined hands. "What I'm saying is, I don't think I can continue to monitor storms. Outside of office hours, that is."

He opened his mouth and gave a small shake of his head.

I licked my lips, my mouth dry. The disappointment on his face was a bitter thing to swallow. "I'll always support your love for storm chasing," I said. "And I'd once dreamed of spending every weekend, every vacation with you. At the bunker, where it's just the two of us in the middle of the storm season in that small bed. It's all I ever wanted."

He was frowning now, shaking his head. "If you want that, why can't we?"

"Because I almost died. And you made me promise last time that I'd consider you before I tried to get myself killed again. So that's what I'm doing." I squeezed his hand. "Seeing you so upset, knowing what I put you through. It made me realise that you were right. I need to consider people other than myself. Which is not something I'm too familiar with, to be honest. I've never had anyone . . ." I lifted his hand to my lips. "So if that means my research days are over—or field trips, at least—then so be it."

"Jeremiah," he murmured.

"It's not a bad thing. I can still study and research, but running out into electrical storms . . ." I shook my head. "Not if it ever hurts you again. I can't do it. And I'm not sad about it. My priorities are quite clear to me now. And my priorities are you, and my work, of course. But standing out in a clearing holding a metal rod to the sky during a storm is now not so appealing."

"Jem," he whispered. "I never meant that you had to stop. I'd never ask you to stop."

"I know. And I would never ask you to stop either. I know you love it, and I know you've had relationships where they've not understood. I'm not like them. I do understand and I want you to keep doing whatever you love. I'll always support you."

"But you won't come with me," he said, frowning.

"Tully, I can't go through this again. I can't put you through this again."

He nodded slowly, his eyes getting that hardened, focused, possibly angry gleam. "See, here's the thing, Jeremiah," he said. "I've been chasing storms my whole life. Since I was a kid, doin' all kinds of crazy shit with my dad and then when I was old enough to do it on my own. And I ain't ever been struck by lightning."

"Neither had I," I countered. "And for the record, I wasn't doing crazy shit. It was a freak electrical discharge. Just because it isn't raining or storming overhead doesn't mean lightning can't strike."

"Exactly," he said. "You just said it. It was a freak accident. There was no way you could have predicted it. You didn't mean for it to happen."

I may have now only just seen the corner I'd painted myself into.

He smiled as if he knew, though it was still a little

sad. "It wasn't like you were out there holding a metal pole up to the sky, actively seeking out a strike point. Not like when you wanted to trek into mangroves holdin' a bunch of metal equipment. Or that time you ran out into a storm to fix your weather station and almost got hit. Those were deliberate acts of stupidity."

I snorted. "Thanks."

"Or the time you saved Casey and Presley. That was deliberate and stupid, but you saved those kids so I'm giving you a pass."

I smiled but he was also helping my point. "All these times are just proof that I need to stop."

"No. It's proof you need to start thinking. So we keep goin' to the bunker, and we can take all the monitoring gear." He leaned in close, his eyes trained on mine. "And we make love on that small bed while the storms rage outside."

My ECG machine beeped.

He looked at it. "Oops."

My nurse appeared like a genie from an ECG bottle. "What did you do?"

Tully got off the bed, his hands behind his back. "Just making sure it still works, that's all. A civic duty, if you will."

She glared at him, then she smiled at me. "Is he bothering you?"

"Yes."

He gasped. "Husband! How could you?"

She looked at me. "There's another visitor waiting out in the hall. I told her there's only one at a time and that you were here."

"Her?" Tully asked. "Mum wasn't coming in till this arvo."

"I can't remember her name," the nurse said. "Tall, older lady, shaved head. Shirt has a dinosaur on it. Was her name Doreen?"

Tully grinned at me. "Our favourite lesbian."

I laughed and it hurt my ribs. "Ow."

He kissed the side of my head. "I'll go get her and she can say hi, and I'll go and get you a proper coffee."

They were both gone, and I barely had time to think about everything Tully had said before he came back with Doreen. "Here he is," Tully said. "Now please talk some sense into him."

"Sense about what?" she asked.

"He doesn't think he should come storm chasing with me anymore," he replied. "Tell him that's a load of shit."

Someone in the ward said something about his language and Tully disappeared behind the curtain, leaving Doreen standing there. She was holding a bag in her hand, wringing the handle.

I'd never seen her look so awkward.

"How ya holdin' up?" she asked.

"Had better days," I replied. "But I'm getting better."

She was still fidgeting with the bag. "Tully said it was a close call."

"Yeah. Lucky he was there."

She nodded. "So you gonna quit or something?"

"What? Quit the office? No." I shook my head. "You can't get rid of me that easily."

She finally smiled. "Well, good. Glad to hear that. They tell me the install's about to start. Some optic cable guys came by to measure something."

Finally.

"Oh, that is good news."

"But don't you worry about none of that. I'll keep 'em on their toes for ya, make sure none of them are slackin' off."

I smiled. "Good. Thank you."

She nodded, looking around awkwardly again. "Couldn't believe it when I heard. I was gonna come in yesterday, but Tully said today might be better."

"Thank you for coming in," I said. "It's a lovely surprise."

She nodded to the balloons. "Lemme guess. Tully gotcha those?"

"Ah, no. His brother."

She nodded as if that made total sense. "Kinda funny."

I smiled at her. "It is."

She winced. "You know I'm not a fan of hospitals."

"I got that impression, yes." It was only then I noticed her shirt. It did indeed have a dinosaur on it. It was pink, white, and orange—the lesbian pride colours—with long eyelashes, and underneath it was the writing *lickalotapus*.

I expected nothing less.

"Love your shirt."

She smiled, for real this time. "Thanks. It's new." Then she only just seemed to remember that she was holding something. "Oh, I got this for you. I got it when

I ordered mine. Was gonna save it for Christmas or a birthday or somethin', but it didn't feel right comin' to see ya and not bring something."

She handed it over. Inside the bag was a shirt, which I could see had the words *I love Dick* written on it and a picture of Dick Van Dyke's face.

I laughed and my ribs twinged. "I love it, thank you."

"No worries." Then she rocked back and forth on her heels, uncomfortable again. "So, uh, did it hurt?"

I didn't mind her questions. She was, after all, a meteorologist. Her curiosity was natural. "I don't remember it. The pain afterwards, yes. When I came to, I guess, for the want of a better word. There was pain. Everywhere."

"Was it a direct hit?"

I shook my head. "Side splash. Got me in the ribs." I lifted my left arm, and she looked and winced.

"Jesus."

"Right near the heart."

"And the Lichtenburg marks?"

"You mean my Lightning McQueen racing flames?"

She smiled at that, but then looked at my torso. "Jesus, Mary, and Joseph. It's unreal. Any exit wounds?"

"A matching pair on the sole of each foot."

She shook her head, seemingly lost for words. "You were lucky, huh?"

"Yes."

"So, no more storm chasin', huh?"

I shrugged. "I don't know. I saw what I put Tully

through, and I can't do that again. I need to think of him now too. I don't think he's happy with my decision, but . . ."

"Give it some time," she said. "It's not so much the storm chasin' you gotta quit. It's the doin' stupid shit like runnin' out in a lightnin' storm that you gotta quit."

I snorted. "Thanks. I'll keep that in mind."

"I'm just sayin', if you love it, if it's part of what makes you *you*, then if you quit, then you're quittin' part of yourself. And that can lead to resentment and if you blame yourself or Tully, or maybe he'll blame you. It ain't good either way."

"What's not good either way?" Tully asked as he walked back in, holding a takeaway coffee cup. "Nurse said they're comin' to put some dye in ya for the echo-thingy ultrasound. I asked if the dye would make you glow in the dark. She said no. But I did ask if the coffee was okay, and yes, you can still drink this." He put the coffee on my table. And then he saw the shirt. He held it up. "Oh my god, this is the best thing I've ever seen. I'm gonna need one in every colour."

"It's not yours," Doreen said. "It's Jeremiah's."

"We share a wardrobe," Tully said. "What's mine is mine and what's his is mine."

Then, because Tully was Tully, he pulled his own shirt off over his head and pulled on the *I love Dick* shirt. He patted it down and grinned right at me. "You like?"

I couldn't stop smiling at him. "I love."

He beamed, giving Doreen one of his grins, and she rolled her eyes.

Tully rolled his other shirt into a ball and shoved it in the bag. "Anyway, the nurse said we gotta go. I'll come back as soon as they let me in." He leaned down and kissed my forehead. "Love you. See you soon."

"Love you too," I said.

He was still beaming, and he laughed when my ECG line stuttered upwards. "Oops."

My nurse appeared like magic again, her glare fixed directly at Tully. "Is your husband being a menace again?"

I saw Doreen do a double take at the word husband, and Tully must have seen it too. He quickly took her arm. "Come on, Dory. Time to go." She managed a wave before they disappeared.

My nurse tsked after him. "Does that grin of his get him whatever he wants?"

I chuckled. "Yes, it does."

She patted my arm. "Okay, let's get you ready for this test. What did we call it?"

"One step closer to going home."

CHAPTER TWELVE
TULLY

Leavin' the hospital without Jeremiah got harder every time. He was gettin' better, and I didn't need a doctor to tell me that. He was brighter, smiled more, talked more, slept less, and didn't wince every single time he moved.

I walked Doreen to the car park and thanked her again for coming to see him. She wasn't the big bad meanie she made herself out to be, though I doubt I'd be calling her Dory again anytime soon.

She threatened a specific kind of bodily harm and then laughed. Not like it was a joke, but in a 'do it again, I dare ya' kinda way.

I wouldn't be tempting that fate any time soon.

Knowing Jeremiah would be busy for an hour or so, I headed to the office. I'd basically abandoned my job in the last few days, so pickin' up some slack while I could was a good idea.

Keepin' busy was too.

I opened my emails, fully expecting a barrage, and I

wasn't disappointed. I'd only got through a handful when Rowan walked past my office, saw me, and stopped.

"Oh hey," he said, coming in. "I didn't think you'd be in this week."

"I'm not here now," I replied. "Just tryin' to make a dent in my inbox."

"Everything okay at the hospital?"

"Yeah, he's just havin' some tests done. I'll go back soon."

He only just seemed to notice my shirt. "Uh, nice shirt."

I laughed. "Thanks. It was Jeremiah's. Now it's mine."

He made a face that said 'Jeremiah would never wear that' but didn't say it out loud. "Ellis said his dad gets in this afternoon."

I inhaled and sighed. "Yep."

"Is that not a good thing?"

"It is." I puffed out my cheeks with another sigh. "Well, I hope it will be. They have a kinda strained relationship. Never been very close."

He nodded slowly and came in to sit in the chair across from me. "It must've been difficult for both of them after Jeremiah's mum died. And I'm not excusing his dad's behaviour at all . . ."

I wasn't sure where he was trying to take this.

"What?"

"I know if it was me, if I were in his shoes, well, I'd like to think . . . If Diah died, I'd like to think it'd make me hold my kids tighter, love them harder. But you just never know. I'd be a forever-changed man too. It'd break me. And I'm pretty sure after seeing what you went through with Jeremiah these last few days, it'd break you too."

I . . . I was speechless.

Rowan shrugged. "And we have a big family that steps up when we need it, and I can't imagine how hard it was for Jeremiah, having no one and growing up like that. I'm sure his father did all he could do to provide for him the best he knew how." He ran his hand through his hair. "I don't know what I'm trying to say."

I wasn't sure either. "Are you okay, Rowan?"

He let out a breathy laugh. I couldn't ever recall seeing him embarrassed, yet here he was. "Yeah, I am. I'm just saying maybe Jeremiah's dad isn't a bad person. And I know you're inclined to be protective of Jeremiah and god help anyone who dares to look at him wrong, but maybe now you can sympathise with his dad a little."

"I wasn't gonna be rude to him."

"I know. I know you wouldn't. But he lost the love of his life, just like you almost lost yours." He shrugged again. "Maybe when we meet him this afternoon, we can show him that Jeremiah—"

"Wait. When *we* meet him?"

"Yeah well, Mum thought it might be nice if we all came around for dinner."

"Oh, did she now?"

"Did you want it to be just you and him at home tonight? With Ellis?"

Oh god. "That's a good point."

He chuckled as he stood up. "I'll bring some duct tape. Just in case."

I snorted. "Thanks."

He walked to the door. "Say hi to Jeremiah for us."

"I will."

He left me to wonder if that wasn't the weirdest conversation I'd ever had with my eldest brother. I'd never been close to him. We'd always been at different stages of our lives and never had much in common.

Until now.

I got through another three emails when Mum found me. She knocked and walked straight in. "Oh, Rowan said you were in."

"In the flesh." I checked my watch. "For another thirty minutes, maybe."

"So I was thinking . . ."

"About dinner? Rowan told me."

She smiled as she sat down. "I thought it might be nice. I know he'll be tired after travelling and he'll want to see Jeremiah, of course. But we can have dinner all ready at your place when you get home, and we'll be gone by eight thirty. How does that sound?"

I wasn't sure . . .

"It'll be nice for him to see how accepted Jeremiah is in our family, don't you think?"

"Well . . ." When she put it like that . . . "I guess."

And Jeremiah will be glad he's not there to witness it.

"Any dietary requirements?"

"Not that I know of. Mum," I said. "He's not the fancy type. Please don't go all out to impress him."

"I won't."

"I just don't want him to think that we're preten-tious or that we think we're too good for them. I don't want Jeremiah's dad to think—"

"Tully, stop stressing about it. I'm sure he'll see you for who you are, and his only concern will be that you treat his son well. Which you do. That's all any parent wants. He'll be fine."

Ellis chose that exact moment to walk into my office. "Oh look, it's my second favourite nut sac."

Mum sighed. "How could anyone ever think we're pretentious?"

I snorted. "Ellis will be on his best behaviour, won't you?"

"For dinner tonight?" He grinned. "Of course."

Oh great.

"You know, maybe tonight's not such a great idea—"

"I know when to behave myself, jeez," he grumbled. "So how was Lightning McQueen this morning?"

I was gonna rebuke him, but honestly, what was the point?

"He was good. He's getting better, though he didn't sleep too well last night." I sighed. "He said he doesn't wanna go storm chasing anymore. He said he doesn't wanna risk gettin' hurt again because of me."

Mum gave me a sad smile. "He's had quite a scare, love. And he saw how it affected you. I'm not surprised he's having second thoughts."

Ellis completely dismissed it. "Oh please. Give him two weeks and he'll be back out there on the patio watching storms with you. He gets that same stupid, excited look on his face you get when thunder starts to roll."

I snorted. "Gee, thanks."

Mum gave a pointed nod to my computer. "You know you can just leave that."

"I know. But it helps to feel productive." I checked my watch again. "I gotta head back soon anyway. I told him I'd be there as soon as they'd let me see him."

"Did you want me to get his dad from the airport?" Ellis asked.

I considered it for half a second. "As much as I don't wanna leave him, I think I should pick him up. Good first impressions and all."

Ellis grinned at me. "Meeting the father-in-law, huh? Are you nervous?"

God yes.

"No."

He snorted. "If you're gonna lie, you need to get better at it."

I let out a puff of air. "Thanks."

Mum stood up, signalling for Ellis to do the same. "You'll be fine, Tully. He'll love you. Come on, Ellis. We're keeping him from getting anything done."

"Do you need me to grab anything for dinner tonight?"

"Not a thing." Mum ushered Ellis out the door. "Give Jeremiah our love. Oh, and Tully?"

"Yeah."

"Before you pick up Jeremiah's father, you might want to reconsider the shirt."

Ellis clearly hadn't paid my shirt any attention. He looked at it now and cracked up laughing, and Mum led him out the door.

I sighed at my now empty office. I hadn't got a lot of work done but they did give me a lot to think about.

I knew Jeremiah was in pain as soon as I walked in. He tried to sit up a little when he saw me, and he gasped and winced.

I took his hand. "What's wrong?"

He shook his head. "Nothing. They just made me move a lot. On my side, and they had to push against my ribs. I'm fine."

I brushed the hair off his forehead. "Can I get you anything?"

He pointed to his lips and pouted.

I laughed and kissed him. "Better?"

"Yes."

I kissed his forehead for good measure. "So what did the docs say?"

"Full report to come, but prelim was good. Nothing worse, slight improvement, rhythm normal and blood flow good."

"That's great news."

He smiled, tired but happy. "It is. He mentioned moving to another ward, but I really just want to go home."

"I want you to come home too. I said I'd hire a full-time nurse, and I mean it. Just for a few days or a week, or however long it takes. At least you'd be home. Mr Percival misses you."

"He does?"

I nodded. "Well, he squawks a lot. I don't speak magpie."

He smiled and squeezed my hand. "I'd like to go home."

"Want me to bust you out? Because I will. I can wear some scrubs and put your sheet over your head, wheel you right out the door. No one would know."

"I think they might."

"Well, I could ask about getting you discharged legitimately, but it's not as much fun."

"I'm supposed to stay off my feet," he said. "I have to be careful of the exit wounds. I'm supposed to be doing leg exercises, which would be fine if my ribs didn't hurt so much."

"Want me to bend your legs for you?"

He raised one tired eyebrow. "I'm almost certain that's not what they had in mind."

I snorted. "That's not what I meant at all. You've got a dirty mind."

He chuckled but his cheeks flushed pink.

I sighed and ran my thumb across his cheekbone. "Blush is my favourite colour on you."

He looked up at me, slow-blinkin'. "That kind of talk isn't helping with my dirty mind."

That made me laugh. "Wanna give that ECG machine a workout?"

He snorted, but then he winced and held his ribs. "Maybe another time."

"I wish I could do something to help."

"You being here helps. It really does."

I kissed his temple. "Can I take you out of this room at least? In a wheelchair?"

He brightened for half a second, like that was the best idea ever, then he sighed. "I'm not sure. I'd have to ask. Maybe when the doctor comes in. If they're taking me to a different ward, I'd imagine they'd want me up and about more than I have been."

"Do your feet still hurt?"

"Not so much."

"I can help you walk. Take you to the bathroom." Then I whispered, "And hold your dick when you pee."

That made him smile. "You might have to shower me too."

"Hell yes I will." The banter was fun but he was getting tired, so I sat in the chair beside him and took his hand. "Well, when we get you home, I'll park you up on the comfy couch with all the snacks and movies you wanna watch."

"And books."

"All the books you want."

"I miss my phone. I miss reading."

"Oh, babe, you should have said." I put my phone on his table. "Use mine, download any books you want."

"I can't take your phone."

"I'll survive. Just until I get you another one."

"Do you even know where my phone is? You said it got fried, right?"

I nodded. "Yeah. It's dead. It didn't like fifty-thousand volts, apparently. We can check the sim card though."

"Same as my watch."

"I'll get you a new one of them too. And a new chest strap. Though it won't be for scientific purposes now. It'll be medical, so I make sure we don't overdo it. I fully expect gold stars though. There's a lot to be said about taking it slow."

He didn't sigh, he didn't argue, he didn't get mad. He just watched me with soft eyes and a warm smile. "I love you," he murmured. "I don't know what I'd do without you."

Just then, the familiar rattle and smell of the lunch trolley came into the ward. "I'm going to feed you some lunch first. And then when they make me leave, what you can do without me is get some sleep. I'll be back after three," I said. "With your dad."

His eyes widened, then he deflated a little. "I forgot."

Standing up, I kissed the side of his head. "Babe, it'll be fine. And you should consider yourself lucky that you're in here, because my parents insisted that he meet my entire family for dinner. At our place. Including Ellis."

"Oh dear."

I nodded. "Exactly."

I WAITED AT THE AIRPORT, LIKE I HAD MANY TIMES BEFORE. Not so long ago waiting for Jeremiah. Now waiting for his father.

I was ignoring the nerves, pretending it wasn't making me feel sick. But I was thinking maybe eating lunch had been a bad idea.

Calm down, Tully. It'll be fine. Everything's gonna be fine.

I'd only ever seen one photo of the man before, but I didn't need it. There was only one man who came through the Arrivals door that could be Jeremiah's dad. No mistaking it.

He was tall and thin, wearing trousers and a white button-down shirt. He had dark grey hair and striking blue eyes.

Not as blue as Jeremiah's, but still . . .

He was simply an older version of Jeremiah himself.

He was scannin' the crowd, nervous and out of place.

"Mr Overton?" I said with a smile. I offered him my hand. "Tully Larson. We spoke on the phone."

He shook my hand. "Oh yes, yes, of course. Uh, thank you for coming to pick me up, and for the ticket, of course."

Seeing that he was as nervous as me made me feel a little better.

"You're more than welcome." I looked at his carry-on bag. "Are we waiting for any more luggage?"

"No, no. Just this."

"Perfect. Then we should get going. Jeremiah's excited to see you." I gestured to the exit.

He gave a nod and we walked out. "Is he . . . is he any better?"

"Much better than he was," I said. "But he's still . . . well, he's still laid up." I got to my car and pressed the button for the boot to open.

He put his carry-on in and wiped his palms on his thighs. "Nice car."

I almost laughed. "You know, Jeremiah looked at it much the same way. I've also got a Jeep that's about twenty years old and he prefers to drive that, but this one has air conditioning."

"Ah, yes. This humidity is no joke."

I opened the passenger door for him and smiled. "Jeremiah said the exact same thing."

I climbed in behind the wheel and getting us out of the car park was a good distraction. I didn't have to worry about what to say for a minute or two, at least.

"Darwin's had a rough time of it," he said as we made our way into traffic. "I tried to catch it on the news, but the Melbourne channels stopped showing it when it wasn't news anymore."

"You saw Jeremiah's interview where he told you he was okay, yeah?"

He furrowed his brow. "Well, yes. Though he probably shouldn't have wasted important resources for that."

It was hard not to smile at him because, my god, he and Jeremiah were so alike. "That news crew owed him. A ten second interview to let you know he was okay was the least they could do."

He scowled before schooling his features. "Yes, with the lightning strike. I saw that too."

"When he saved those two kids?" I nodded. "He's a bit of a hero in this town."

He watched the passing scenery for a few long seconds: the still-damaged buildings, the construction work. "It didn't help him much this last time though."

I withheld my sigh. I wanted to say *so* much, but knew I had to bite my tongue.

"There was no storm when he was hit," I offered gently. "No thunder, no rain. He wasn't reckless or foolish. It was just a freak accident."

He nodded solemnly, his mouth a grim line. "I've heard that before."

And there it was.

A painful truth that he'd lived through this before.

As simple as that.

We drove in silence the rest of the way. There was nothing I could say, nothing I could add.

As we pulled into the hospital car park, I saw him in a different light. Yep, he was a lot like Jeremiah—that was true—but there were differences too.

His father was gaunt, the lines on his face were ingrained with almost thirty years of grief. There was a dark cloud over him, and though he'd smiled when I first met him, I could see now that it was just a conscious effort at an expected facial expression.

Whereas Jeremiah still laughed, he still had light in his eyes. His father didn't.

I had to wonder if he'd smiled at all since Jeremiah's mother died.

And Rowan's words came back to me.

"If Diah died, I'd like to think it'd make me hold my kids tighter, love them harder. But you just never know. I'd be a forever-changed man, too. It'd break me. And I'm pretty sure after seeing what you went through with Jeremiah these last few days, it'd break you too."

And I knew exactly what Rowan had said was true.

Jeremiah's father broke the day his wife died. I didn't know what kind of man he was before, but I'd hazard a guess that the light inside him died alongside her. And I understood, I could sympathise. Because Jeremiah almost died and it damn near almost broke me too.

So yeah, like Rowan had also said, I could maybe sympathise with Jeremiah's dad a little.

I pulled into a parking spot and shut off the engine. "Let's go see him. He was sleeping when I left him, so hopefully he's had a good rest."

Mr Overton gave another nod and we headed inside. His nervousness ratcheted up a notch with every step, and he stopped dead when he realised I was taking him to the ICU.

"ICU?"

"Yep. They're hoping to move him out today. He had some tests done this mornin' and he was waiting to hear back from the doc."

"Is he . . . can he . . . ?" He looked considerably more gaunt now. "I should have asked before now. When you said on the phone that he wasn't well . . ."

I put my hand on his arm. "He's okay. He's going to make a full recovery. He's talking, eating, and drinking.

He's still got his sense of humour. They're talkin' about getting him up and walking. He's just here because of his heart."

"His heart . . . ?"

Oh god.

"Yeah, the high voltage gave his ticker a jumpstart. So he's hooked up to machines that measure every beat. It's mostly precautionary," I added, trying to placate him a little.

Jeez.

I sucked at this.

Oh . . .

And then I remembered something else.

Ah, hell. Here goes nothing.

"Oh, and uh, yeah, before you go in," I hedged, lookin' around to see who might be within earshot. "The hospital might be under the impression that Jeremiah and I are married?"

He stared.

"We're not," I added quickly. "It's just so that I can be here with him, ya know? Makes it easier, that's all."

His brows did that unimpressed thing again, his mouth a disappointed thin line. "Right."

So that went well.

"Okay, let's not keep him waiting."

I got him signed in and led him into the ward. I held the curtain for him and followed him in.

Jeremiah was still in bed, and it looked as if there'd been some attempt to brush his hair. As soon as he saw his dad, he tried to sit up straighter and winced immediately. "Dad," he said. There was hope in his eyes, and for a brief second, I got a glimpse of a small boy who'd have given anything in the world to make his father happy.

His dad took one look at him, nodded, and began to cry.

CHAPTER THIRTEEN

JEREMIAH

Seeing my father upset, seeing him show any kind of emotion at all, took me by such surprise I wasn't sure how to react.

Seeing him cry made me cry too.

Instant tears, my heart heavy, a lump in my throat.

I tried to reach for him but it hurt my ribs, and he quickly took my hand. "Sorry, son," he said, wiping his cheeks, trying to compose himself. "Just got a little shock to see you, that's all."

I'd never seen my father cry. Not ever.

"It's okay, Dad," I said.

Tully wheeled my table over closer to me, and there were now tissues on it. He kissed the side of my head. "I'll just be out in the hall."

I watched him leave, the curtain swishing after him. Dad stood there, uncertain and clearly not sure what to say. "He seems a nice fellow."

I laughed, still teary. "He is." I still had hold of his

hand and reluctantly let it go. "Take a seat. How was your flight?"

He sat down as if the seat would bite him. "I'm sorry about before," he said quietly. "I just . . . I don't know what came over me."

"It's okay, Dad," I said again. "I've missed you. I'm really glad you made the trip."

He shifted in his seat. "Yes, well . . . Tully insisted I come. He paid for it, which I didn't expect him to do that, and I can pay him back the money."

"He'd probably be offended if you tried. And he is insistent. If you'd have said no, he'd probably have gone to Melbourne to bring you up here himself." I smiled. "He's a good man, Dad. He saved my life."

His eyes cut to mine. "He, uh, he said you weren't doing too well. When he first called me. He said he thought it best if I make the trip."

I nodded. "Yeah. It was pretty scary."

His gaze bored into mine. That hesitancy, that awkward habit of his to not hold eye contact was gone. "Lightning, huh?"

I sighed, dreading this conversation that we had to have. "Yes. I know."

"I almost lost you both to it. Do you know what that would've done to me?"

I tried to keep my breathing low, my heart rate down, but damn. Being hooked up to every machine made it hard to disguise. My blood pressure began to rise, and I knew my nurse was just a few seconds away.

"I'm sorry, Dad. I didn't mean for this to happen. I didn't want this—"

And there she was. Breezed in around the curtain and ignored my father completely. She had one hand on my arm, the other pressing the machine. "Jeremiah, my darling, what are we doing to your BP? Are you trying to stay here in the ICU?"

"Sorry, I—"

Dad stood up. "I should go," he said. "I didn't realise my being here—"

"No, Dad. Stay. Please. My research is over," I blurted out. "I'm done. I can't do this again. I can't put Tully through this again. Or you."

Dad stood there, stunned. Disbelieving. "But your work. All those years you put into it."

"It doesn't matter. None of it matters."

He shook his head. "Jeremiah."

My nurse patted my arm. "Keep your heart rate down," she said, then gave my father a parting glare as she left.

Neither of us said anything for a few moments.

"I'm staying in meteorology," I said. "I love my job and I've done good work here, Dad. The people here are great. They like me, they respect me. But my field research is over. I don't need data or statistics on keraunopathy or even keraunomedicine, because I know all I need to know."

He looked at the machines, the curtain, then finally at me. "I don't want you to give up on your dreams. As much as I don't like it or understand it." He shook his head. "You've dedicated your whole life to . . ." He waved his hand at me. "To this."

"And it almost killed me."

He sat back down, and a blanket of acceptance settled over us.

"What will you do?" he asked.

"My job. That won't change." I sighed. "And I will look at my medical records, at the data. There were brain scans and ECGs, et cetera, and maybe one day I'll compare statistics. But my days of chasing lightning in some self-serving attempt to beat it are done."

"What about Tully?" he asked quietly. "I thought you said he enjoyed it as well, that it was something you did together."

"It is. And if he wants to go, then maybe I'll go with him." I swallowed hard. I knew I would, as much as it scared me. Because it mattered to Tully and he shouldn't give up part of who he was to be with me, like Doreen had said. I didn't want him to resent me. So I would go, but I would be careful, like Tully was. "But no more reckless behaviour. I can admit to being reckless and foolish before. It was inconsiderate of me, and I can see that now. I need to think about people other than myself. Like him, and you." I reached for his hand, and hesitantly, he gave it to me. "I'm sorry, Dad. If I ever let you down. Or if I ever disappointed you. Or made you worry."

"Jeremiah," he said, shaking his head.

"Please, Dad. Listen. I had a real wake-up call. And maybe Tully taught me how to say what I feel. I should have said this long before now. I'm sorry if my studies ever caused you concern. And moving forward, I will try to be a better son. I want you to know that I appreciate everything you ever did for me. All the hours you worked, everything you provided. I know you did that for me."

He shook his head again, his chin wobbling. "I tried to make it enough. I couldn't give you what other kids had. I know that."

"It was more than enough, Dad. We got by just fine."

Another tear escaped his eye and he quickly wiped it away. "We did, huh. We got by okay. You grew up to be someone your mum would have been proud of." He sniffled and his eyes welled with tears. "And I'm proud of you too."

I squeezed his hand and swallowed back my tears. "Mum would be proud of you too. It wasn't easy, but here we are."

He took a tissue and wiped at his fresh tears. "Here we are."

With another squeeze of my hand, he let go and sat down. He took a moment to compose himself and to take some deep breaths. This wasn't an easy conversation for us, but I'd said what I needed to say.

And he'd returned the sentiment, which was new ground for us both. I felt as if a weight had been lifted off my shoulders. Did my father and I have a perfect relationship? No. Would we ever? Probably not.

But we were us, and we were going to be fine. I intended to include him more, involve him more. Even if it was a weekly phone call, or maybe I could teach him how to do video calls.

"So," he said. "Tully's a nice young man."

"He is, Dad. I love him."

He blinked in surprise. "Right, yes. Well, I'm glad. I'm happy for you. He, uh, he has a nice car."

He's trying. He's actually trying to talk about my boyfriend.

Another first.

I chuckled, my heart warm. I half expected one of those damn machines to beep, but it didn't.

"He's great, Dad. He's kind and thoughtful and generous. He loves with his whole heart. He has a great family; they've been very welcoming to me. Taken me in like one of their own."

He nodded slowly. "That's . . . that's nice." He shifted in his seat and fidgeted with his hands. "I'm happy for you."

"You'll see what I mean when you meet them tonight."

"When I . . . tonight?"

I snorted. "Ah, yes. Um, about that." I let out a slow breath. "They're holding a welcoming dinner for you at Tully's house tonight. It's only casual and what you're wearing is perfectly fine." I said that because I knew he would ask. "But I should include a fair warning. There's a lot of them and they're loud. But they're amazing people, and they will make a fuss over you, and it's honestly less painful if you just let them."

I smiled at the look of horror on his face. It was where I inherited the same look from. "Oh."

"Mrs Larson promised everyone would be gone by eight thirty. Or so Tully said."

The curtain pulled back and my doctor stood there with Tully behind him. The doctor was smiling and

Tully was grinning, so I assumed it was good news. Though Dad stood up, wringing his hands again.

"It's okay, Dad. It's good news." I looked at Tully and he nodded. I met the doctor's eyes. "You're moving me to a different ward?"

"The results of the TTE are good, and the blood-work's good. Cardiac enzymes are back to normal levels."

Thank God.

"That is good news."

The doctor nodded, then gave Tully a smile. "As much as someone wants you to go home today, I think one or two more nights in a different ward would be best. We need to get you up and moving, make sure the pressure on your feet doesn't affect those burn wounds and that other bodily functions are okay. The tests for your renal enzymes also came back clear, so once we get you using the bathroom on your own, walking on your own, then you'll be free to go home."

Tully was just about to burst. "Did you hear that? He said *home*. You just gotta stand up and pee."

The doctor closed his eyes for a second. "That's not—"

I put my arm out. "Tully, help me up."

Tully laughed and came straight over. "How about we lower the bed first and get you sitting up with your feet on the floor? See how you feel?"

I nodded. "Perfect."

My ribs twinged, but it helped if I kept my arm tucked against my side. But I managed to sit up with my feet on the floor.

Tully kept his hand on my shoulder. "How does that feel?"

I glanced at the monitors to see if they'd betray me. Thankfully they didn't. "Feels good."

The doctor sighed and gave my dad a smile. "There's no greater motivator than the word *home*." Then he looked at me. "How about we get your catheter out?"

Having a catheter removed wasn't a great deal of fun, but being free of it was a big relief.

One step closer to going home.

I sat on the edge of the bed again, my feet on the floor, and Tully and my nurse held onto me while I stood up.

My dad stood there, looking all kinds of helpless, but he smiled when I did.

I managed a few small steps but I couldn't stand for long, and while the idea of going home sounded like heaven, I knew realistically another night at least in hospital was probably a good idea.

I was so unbelievably tired.

That small amount of exertion had taken a lot out of me, and my nurse kept a close eye on every machine I was hooked up to. By the time I'd been moved to a normal ward, I could barely keep my eyes open.

I was still attached to one heart monitor, but nothing else.

One step closer to going home.

Tully put his hand to my cheek. "Jem, you need some sleep," he said gently.

Given he'd done and said this in front of my father, I

should have been embarrassed. The old me would have been horrified, and my dad looked as if he'd witnessed something incredibly private.

But all I could do was smile. I held Tully's hand to my face and sighed. "I am tired."

"Then we'll go," Tully said. "And we'll be back bright and early tomorrow, and we'll practice more walking. As much as I want you to come home, we're not gonna rush it. However long it takes, okay?"

I nodded, exhausted. "Okay."

He kissed my temple. "Love you."

Again, in front of my father.

"Love you too," I said, fighting to keep my eyes open. "Love you too, Dad."

First time in my life I'd ever said those words.

I wanted so much to see his face, but my eyes betrayed me. After a long beat of silence, his warm hand squeezed my arm. "Sleep well, son."

I was so happy, even in my almost-asleep state.

Then Tully's voice, fading as they walked away, said, "So I need to explain something before we get to my place. I have a brother, Ellis . . ."

I WOKE UP JUST AFTER FIVE IN THE MORNING, HUNGRY AND determined.

I was going home today.

I knew it would be tough, and I would need to take precautions and be sensible. But I was determined to get the all-clear from my doctor.

I'd missed the family dinner last night—well, Tully's family and my father—and I didn't want to miss another thing.

I was certain everything went well. I knew my father would be overwhelmed but gracious, and of course the Larsons would take the very best care of him.

I just wished I'd been there to see it.

So, if I was going home today, I needed an early start.

I had a new nurse now, along with the new room, new ward, new everything. When I buzzed for an attendant, a middle-aged, robust woman came in with a smile. "Everything okay, Mr Overton?"

I didn't bother correcting her on my title. "Yes. I'd like to use the bathroom and perhaps have a shower. Before the breakfast rush, if that's okay. It's been an embarrassing number of days since I last showered." I tried sitting up on the edge of the bed, my feet on the floor. "My . . . husband . . . and my father will be here first thing and I'd like to be presentable. And preferably not have swamp breath."

She laughed. "Then let's get you showered and minty fresh."

And if I thought having a hot shower after five days at the bunker was heaven, then this shower was out of this world.

Even if I was sitting in a chair stark naked and had a nurse checking in on me.

That hot water, the razor, the soap, the toothpaste . . .

Heaven. On. Earth.

But by the time Tully and Dad came in, I was sitting

up in bed, with freshly washed hair, a new gown, eating some wholemeal toast.

Tully did a double take when he saw me. He put a bag beside the bed and looked me up and down. "Uh, excuse me, while you're incredibly good looking and the, yes, dress is flattering, I'm looking for Jeremiah Overton."

I snorted at his term for my hospital gown.

"Who is this new man?" he said, kissing my head.

I laughed. "I found him in the shower. It was the best shower of my life."

Tully was very much about to comment on that—in all likelihood something rude—but I made a point of ignoring him and looked at my dad instead. "Morning," I said. He was standing at the end of my bed and smiling, which made me incredibly happy to see. "How was dinner last night?"

He glanced briefly at Tully but then back at me. "It was very nice."

I looked between them. "What was the look for? What happened?"

Tully laughed. "Nothing. It was all great. Mum made sure everyone was gone by half eight and Ellis was on his best behaviour."

Dad smiled, nodding. "I thought Ellis was polite and well-mannered."

"Well-mannered?" I studied Tully's face for a hint of humour. "No name-calling, no wrestling, no belching? No threats of grievous bodily harm?"

Tully laughed. "The threats of bodily harm were all given before we arrived. Mum made it pretty clear. Ellis was good. And when everyone left, he ducked out to see Grace."

"Oh? Things going well, I hope?"

Tully clucked his tongue. "We all hope. For all our sakes." Then he rubbed my arm, my shoulder. "You feelin' okay today? How are your feet?" He took a look at my soles. "They look good. Was standing and walking okay?"

"It was manageable. I'm just letting them dry properly. Apart from my feet, showering and walking took considerable effort and energy, and I will be taking a nap soon, I think. But . . ." I met Tully's gaze. "I'd really like to go home today."

Tully grinned and picked up the bag. "I packed you some things, in case today was the day." Then he looked at my dad, then at me. "I'll go grab us a coffee. Mr Overton, black with one sugar?"

"That'd be great, thank you."

He gave me a smiley kiss on the temple and left me alone with my father.

"So, tell me honestly, how was last night?"

Dad was still smiling, not something I saw on him very often. "It was very nice. Honestly. They're all lovely people. I mean, there were a lot of kids and noise. But the madness is part of the charm, right?"

I chuckled. "It is."

"And his house . . ."

That made me laugh. "I know. It's very big and expensive."

"I take it they have a lot of money," he said quietly. "Not that they paraded it or anything. Actually, they're very down-to-earth people. But, well, you know . . ."

And I *did* know. When you grew up and lived with only the bare essentials, and sometimes not even that, someone with money was easy to spot. And it wasn't just the flash cars or expensive jewellery. A lot of it was behaviour that came from a privilege they weren't even aware of.

"I do know," I replied. "When I first met Tully, he wore old clothes and drove an old banged-up Jeep. Then he took me to his house. It was quite the separation from who I assumed he was. But he's just a normal guy, Dad. They all are."

He shrugged one shoulder. "They said the family business was shipping. Not sure what that means."

"You know the shipping containers and freighters with the knight's helmet?"

He nodded, then his eyes went wide. "*Those* Larsons?"

I chuckled. "Yes. Don't worry, I almost died when he took me to his office and I realised. He'd never told me who his family was. He just said he works in imports and exports. Which isn't a lie. They just don't flaunt it. Actually, I don't think it even occurs to Tully to flaunt it."

Dad was still taken aback. "Well, I never . . . I had no idea."

I smiled and patted his hand. "Proof that they're just normal people."

He nodded, then remembered something. "Oh, I met your bird, Mr Percival. Cheeky thing he is."

"He is." I was glad to be able to rest my head on the bed. I'd done a lot this morning and was already tired again, even though it was barely 7:30 am. "He's a real character."

"Want me to put your bed down a bit?" he asked, concerned. "You can close your eyes for a bit."

"Maybe later," I said. "I'm glad you're here."

His eyes met mine briefly before he looked away again, embarrassed. "I'm glad I'm here too."

"How long are you staying for?"

"Three days. It's all I could get off work."

He'd always worked so hard, and it helped make up my mind. "I really need to go home today."

Tully came in with a tray of coffees and a smile that made my heart thump. I glanced at the machine; it didn't beep but there was a spike.

It made Tully laugh. "I'm definitely gonna get us one of these machines. Do you think they'll let us keep this one?"

"Highly unlikely."

He handed us our coffees. "Yours is on skim milk," he said. "We're heart-healthy people now."

Oh good lord. "Are you going to police every single thing I eat and drink for the rest of my life?"

He grinned. "That's the plan."

I hadn't meant for the *rest of my life* to imply anything, but the gleam in his eye and the softness of his tone implied exactly that.

Then he startled, as if he'd just remembered something. He picked up the bag and took out a shirt. "Your leaving-hospital shirt."

It was the *I love Dick* shirt.

Because of course it was.

He turned it around to show my father, whose eyeballs almost fell out of his head. "Oh my."

Tully just laughed, no shame, not much decorum either. "Today's the best day ever."

CHAPTER FOURTEEN
TULLY

Jeremiah's dad was so much like Jeremiah it wasn't funny.

Composed, quiet, always-thinking, assessing, and seriously introverted. Smart, too. But he was also courteous and kind.

And under that hard exterior was a big squishy marshmallow.

I hadn't expected him to burst into tears when he first saw Jeremiah in hospital. To be honest, I think his outward show of emotion surprised everyone, himself included.

But it warmed my heart to see.

I was only too happy to leave them alone for some time to talk. Finally, twenty-something years too late, but better late than never.

The Jeremiah that woke up in hospital was a new man. After almost dying twice—first when he was struck by lightning and the second time when his arrythmia damn near flatlined him—he was determined to say what he felt.

He'd told me he loved me. Several times, now. And he'd said it in front of other people. Even his father.

Like he'd been given a second chance at life and wasn't gonna waste a minute.

He told his dad that he loved him too.

Shame it took nearly dying to do it, but wow, what a transformation.

I guess getting struck by lightning would do that.

But his father . . .

If I had to guess what Jeremiah's father was gonna be like, I'd have imagined him exactly as he was.

Stoic, unsure of people, unassuming, and happy to blend into the background.

After all, how far could the apple fall from the tree?

But there he was with my family, where he was the guest of honour, thrown out of his comfort zone by kids running around the house, adults chatting and laughing, a mountain of food, and my parents who put him at ease.

Dad spoke to him about AFL, and Mum talked to him about inconsequential everyday things. They were pros at this type of thing; making people feel at home, showing kindness and charm that made Mr Overton feel right at home.

He was a factory worker and had been for thirty-plus years. He'd lived in the same house in Melbourne all that time. He never mentioned Jeremiah's mother, and perhaps he didn't have to. The sadness in him was in his eyes, and I remembered what Rowan had said.

He clearly remembered too, because when we were at the BBQ on the patio, he handed me a beer. He didn't say anything, just gave me a smile and a nod—perhaps telling me I'd done the right thing by having Mr Overton stay, by having a family dinner, and by truly understanding why he was the way he was. Then he'd clapped my shoulder and went back to refereeing his kids' game of Twister.

I couldn't have imagined that I'd have found common ground with Rowan either, but through this whole ordeal, he'd been everything I'd needed him to be. Maybe he always had been, and I'd just been too immature and self-absorbed to see it.

Yeah, maybe I'd learned a valuable lesson too.

"Whatcha thinking?" Jeremiah asked.

I must have zoned out, because he and his father were watching me.

"Not much. Just between cyclones and lightning strikes, I think I'm done with life lessons for a good while. Ready to just coast through for a bit, where everything is cosy and boring."

"Cosy and boring sounds great," Jeremiah said, squeezing my hand.

"How much longer till the doctor comes?"

"Five minutes since you asked last time."

I groaned like the child I was, apparently. "I'm gonna go look for him."

I stood up just as the door opened and the doctor walked in . . . pushing a wheelchair.

"Yay!"

Yeah. I actually said yay.

I wasn't even remotely embarrassed.

"Sorry to keep you waiting," the doctor said. "I believe it's discharge o'clock."

I helped Jeremiah to his feet and eased him into the wheelchair. "Do you feel okay?"

He smiled up at me, tired but *so* happy to be leaving. "Yeah."

The doctor looked at Jeremiah's shirt. "Nice shirt."

Jeremiah rolled his eyes and gestured to me, like it explained everything.

I put my hand to my heart. "I happen to be a very big fan of dick."

"Van Dyke," Jeremiah added. "You forgot the Van Dyke."

I snorted, because I absolutely did not forget it, and poor Mr Overton clutched the bag and the balloons, offering the doctor an apologetic smile.

The doc laughed, then handed Jeremiah a clear bag with several bottles of pills and what looked like scripts. "We'll see you back in two weeks. Keep a diary of your bpm and blood pressure. Don't forget."

"He won't," I said. "I drew up a chart for that kind of thing. It has colour-coded stars and everything."

Jeremiah pressed his lips together and sighed. "I'll keep a diary. Thank you, doctor."

He tried to wheel himself out. "Hey," I said, grabbing the handles. "Let me do that."

We left the hospital and I wheeled him into the sunshine outside. He closed his eyes and tilted his face toward the warmth. "Oh, that feels so good."

I gave him a moment to enjoy it. "Ready to go

home? The car's just there."

He nodded and let me help him into the passenger seat, then he let me help him get out and into the house. Then I helped him onto the couch. I brought him a blanket, a tray with drinks and low-sodium snacks and some fruit, and the remote control. "Use the downstairs bathroom and don't try climbing those stairs without me, okay?" I checked the blinds. "Are these open enough? Would you like them closed?"

Jeremiah chuckled. "Tully, I'm fine, thank you. Everything is perfect."

I took Mr Percival out of his cage and he quickly perched himself on my finger, squawking that it was about damn time. I walked him over to Jeremiah. "Here's this little guy. He missed you." Mr Percival agreed by swooping to the couch, then hopping along to Jeremiah as he chorused his happy magpie song.

Jeremiah laughed when Mr Percival hopped onto his shoulder and pecked at his neck and then tried to steal some sliced apple.

"Ah, it's good to be home," Jeremiah said. He was tired, that was pretty obvious, but he hadn't stopped smilin' yet.

I didn't miss the way his dad caught the word home and his understanding of what it meant.

This was Jeremiah's home now.

This house. Darwin.

Me.

His dad joined him on the couch, and he smiled at the silly bird who was trying to steal more apple.

I decided now was a good time as any. And I knew

Jeremiah would probably be mad but . . . "So I got you something," I said.

Jeremiah watched me as I came around the couch, holding a white Apple bag and a brown paper bag.

I sat on the coffee table in front of him. "And you're not allowed to be mad because of your blood pressure and heart rate, so . . ."

His gaze went from the Apple bag to my face. "What did you do?"

I handed it to him. "Technically, Ellis bought it. I mean, I asked him to and it was my card, but he did the buying, so you have to be mad at him and not me."

He pulled out the first box. It was a new phone. And a new watch.

"Yours were fried," I said, now giving him the brown paper bag. "The hospital gave these to me. And the clothes you were wearing. But I thought you might like to see these."

Inside were his old phone and watch and the chest strap.

"None of them work anymore. And the guy at the Apple store said the phone was actually fried. As in, some of it was melted on the inside. He wanted to know if it'd been microwaved." I shrugged. "Ellis said it was. Pretty much. Yeah."

Jeremiah was quiet as he turned his old phone over in his hand, inspecting it.

"Even the sim card was fried," I added. "I couldn't get your number reissued on a new sim because you weren't with me, so you'll have a new number now."

He nodded, then met my gaze. "Thank you."

"At least those news reporters won't be calling you now."

He smiled ruefully. "True."

Then he looked at the watch, at the dirty wristband, at the black screen. He tried to turn it on and sighed when nothing happened.

He took out the chest strap, and without even looking at it, he put it on the couch beside him. "Didn't buy another one of these?" he asked. There was a spark of humour in his eyes.

I grinned at him. "It's on back order."

He gave me a tired smile until his dad picked up the old phone. "Must have been a hell of a zap to fry a phone. And a watch," Mr Overton said quietly. "You were very lucky, huh?"

"Yeah," Jeremiah whispered. His eyes cut to mine and he smiled. "Very lucky indeed."

He could barely keep his eyes open, so I moved the tray of food and put the blanket over him. "Get some sleep."

He nodded, his eyes already closed, and two seconds later, he was out.

I carried the tray into the kitchen and Mr Overton followed me. He was nervous and clearly had something to say. I gave him time to put his thoughts in order.

"I never thanked you," he said, fidgeting his hands, then folding his arms, then uncrossing them again. "It would have been a very different story if not for you. You were there with him when it happened, and he told me you saved his life."

"I was with him. I dunno if I saved his life, but I put in the call for medevac." I shuddered at the memory. "It scared the hell outta me, not gonna lie."

"You love him very much," he said. It wasn't a question. "I can see that."

Jesus. This was not the conversation I expected to be having with his father.

"I do."

He smiled sadly. "I'm glad." Then he swallowed hard and kept his gaze fixed on the ocean views out the window. "He spent his whole life studying, reading, researching. He was never a very sociable child. I worried that was my fault. I worked shiftwork and he was home alone a lot. And when he first told me he liked men, I worried even more for him."

Ah, shit.

"I thought he'd be destined to be alone like me, and I didn't want that for him. I wanted him to have a family, and to know what love was." He turned to face me, making eye contact for a second before glancing away, grimacing a smile. This wasn't easy for him to say, but with a deep breath, he continued. "I needn't have worried, because he has that with you. All of it. Everything I wanted for him. He has that here."

Hmm. *Here.*

"He's a long way from home," I offered. "But what if we come to Melbourne once a year? And you can come here any time you'd like and stay here for as long as you want. Just give me the dates and I'll make it happen. Jeremiah would like that. I've only been to

Melbourne once. It was a while ago now. Maybe we could catch a footy match."

He smiled genuinely then. "That'd be nice. I'd like that too."

We were quiet then, and I wasn't sure what to say. He'd come all this way to learn that he'd very nearly lost his son the same way he'd lost his wife, and now he was losing him to me.

"He's happier here," he said eventually. "In Darwin. He was never really happy where he was. As if he was constantly going against the grain. His colleagues were a contentious bunch. He never got along with them."

"They were a bunch of arseholes who never appreciated him." He looked at me, startled, and all I could do was shrug. "It's true."

He smirked and was quiet again, his gaze out to sea. "Do you . . . do you ever get sick of the view?"

I laughed. "Never."

"Can't say I would either."

I'D NOT REALISED JUST HOW MUCH I'D MISSED SLEEPING next to Jeremiah until I helped him into bed, sliding in beside him, holding him tight. His head was on my chest, my arms around him, and something settled in my bones.

Something that felt like coming home.

"I missed you so much," I murmured. It was late and he'd tried to stay awake after dinner, but he'd dozed on the couch again until I'd helped him upstairs and into bed. "I missed this so much."

He hummed. "Doctor said no sex for a while. Nothing arduous, anyway."

I snorted. "So having competitions as to who can get the highest heart rate is out?"

"I think I won that game."

I gave him a squeeze and kissed the top of his head. "I don't care about the sex," I admitted. "It'll happen when you're ready. I'm just glad you're here. Lyin' in bed with you like this is enough for me."

He kissed my pec. "I'm glad because laying here is about all I'm capable of doing."

I chuckled. "I love you."

He sighed and nuzzled in a little closer. "I love you too. I'm so thankful for you." His voice got slower, quieter, as he drifted off to sleep. "Every little thing. Love every little thing."

I kissed his forehead this time and smiled at the ceiling. "Love every little thing about you too."

<hr>

WATCHING JEREMIAH TALK WITH HIS DAD AND WATCHIN' them smile made me happy in ways I couldn't describe.

Was their entire relationship magically fixed overnight? No. But it was a really good fucking start.

Even when he had to say goodbye to his father at the airport, Jeremiah was still smiling. I mean, he was kinda sad to see him go—and they had hugged goodbye—but when I got him into the car after we'd watched the plane leave, he let his head fall back on the headrest and he gave me a smile.

"You okay?"

"Yeah." He held out his hand, which I was quick to take. "I am. You know, I think we'll be okay."

I kissed his knuckles. "I think you will be too."

"And you and me," he added. "I think we'll be okay too."

"You bet your arse we will be."

He snorted. "Can we drive past my office?"

"You sure?"

He nodded with a tired smile. "Yeah. I just wanna see it."

"Okay."

So I drove him to his office. The gate was open, Doreen's bike was under the carport, and a utility van was parked alongside it. It looked like an electrician's van, with ladders and gear on top.

Doreen came out and grinned when she saw it was us. Her shirt had a picture of a cat-shaped bottle with the words *pussy liquor* on it. I got out of my car laughing. "Possibly my favourite shirt yet."

She looked down at it. "It's a ripper, ain't it?" Then she looked at Jeremiah. "What are you doin' here?"

"Just thought I'd call past. I'm not staying." He nodded toward the van. "Work's started, I see."

"Early days. But yeah, he's fixin' something to do with the mains and a new transformer." She shook her head and shrugged. "Needed a full upgrade for your new computers and shit."

Jeremiah was obviously pleased to hear this. "Thank you for being here. I should be back at work soon."

"Uh," I objected. "The doc said two weeks."

"Yes, two weeks until full-time work. He said nothing about calling in and checking on progress. It's not like I can help them or do anything."

"You just take it easy," Doreen said. "I can come and open a gate for 'em. It's not like I'm busy these days."

"And I do appreciate that—"

"Are you arguin' with me, son?"

He sighed. "No."

She gave a victorious nod. "Good."

I coughed to cover my laugh, and Jeremiah took his phone from his pocket. "I have a new number, if you should need to call me."

"Lemme grab mine," she said, disappearing back inside.

Phone numbers all sorted and a quick update on the street—Arty was still a stubborn old goat, and work had started on Casey and Presley's house—it was time for Jeremiah to go home.

"I wish I wasn't so tired," he grumbled.

"I know, babe. But you're doin' better every day. We'll get you situated on the couch and you can take it easy. I'll make us an early dinner." I helped him inside. "How does homemade pizzas sound? I got those pita bases and low-fat cheese."

He snorted. "They sounded good until the low-fat cheese part."

Ellis met us in the living room. He was just heading somewhere. "Is that dinner about tonight?"

"Yeah, homemade pizzas. Why?"

He grimaced, blushing a little. "Well, I asked Grace if she wanted to come over for dinner tonight."

I grinned at him. "Oh, that sounds very . . . domestic. Will she be staying the whole night?"

His eyes narrowed at me. "Listen, nut sac—"

I laughed. "I'm just stirrin' ya. That's good news, Ellis. I'm glad you're sorting things out with her."

He studied me for a long beat. "Can you not bring any of that shit up in front of her? About how I was a dick to her before? Or try to embarrass me. Or her." He clenched his teeth. "I swear to god, Tully, if you embarrass her—"

"I'll be on my best behaviour." I gave him a salute. "Promise."

"I'll make sure he's well-behaved," Jeremiah said.

Ellis sighed. "I'm going to grab a few things. Need anything for pizzas?"

"Garlic bread and real cheese would be great," Jeremiah said as he walked toward the couch.

"Babe," I started. "You need to watch your heart."

"Garlic bread and real cheese would make my heart happy," he mumbled. "And maybe it will give me energy for later."

I stared at the back of his head.

Did he just . . . ?

"Did you just imply . . . ? Jeremiah!" In front of my brother.

Dear god.

Ellis snorted. "Pretty sure he did, yeah."

Okay then. "Well," I allowed. I nodded to Ellis. "Get him garlic bread and real cheese."

He laughed as he walked to the door. "Oh, it's supposed to storm tonight," he called out before he left.

Hmm.

I jumped on the couch with Jeremiah, snuggling right in so we'd both fit, and I pulled the blanket over us. "Did you hear that? It's supposed to storm tonight."

His eyes stayed closed, he rubbed my back, and the corner of his mouth lifted ever so slightly. "Perfect night to stay indoors."

"You, me, and pizza," I said with a sigh. "And a storm outside. Sounds perfect to me too."

He was quiet for a long beat. "I want to watch storms with you," he murmured. "But I'm not ready to go out in them yet."

I gave him a squeeze. "It's okay, Jem."

"I can have both, right?" he whispered.

Oh my god, yes. "You sure can have both."

"What you said was true. And Doreen. She said the same thing. I can still go storm watching with you. But I'm done being reckless. Not with my heart, and not with yours."

I sighed happily. "That's all I ever wanted."

EPILOGUE

TWO YEARS LATER - TULLY

Paul and Derek's camp had been lucky to escape any real damage during Cyclone Hazer. They were far enough out not to be in its direct path, and had sustained minimal damage.

Thank god.

Pulling up at their camping ground gave me just as much of a thrill as it always did. Even more, probably, now that Jeremiah was with me. We'd come at the beginning of the wet season last year too.

That trip had been Jeremiah's first true outing back in the furore.

Almost ten months after his brush with lightning, he'd wanted to come to the bunker with me. He was scared and he never set foot outside the bunker as soon as there was a cloud in the sky, but he was there with me.

And that was all I ever wanted.

I didn't need him to be a scientist out here. I just

needed him to be happy—and being out here made him happy.

So now we were back, two years after the lightning strike. We had enough gear to last us a week, but if we had to leave earlier, then so be it. The weather was supposed to be warm and humid with afternoon storms.

Perfect.

And my secret, my surprise, the small box in my duffel bag felt like a large elephant in the Jeep with us. I wanted to tell him . . . I wanted to show him . . .

"You good?" Jeremiah asked.

I shut off the engine and gave him a smile. "I'm great."

Paul came out, holding two large containers stacked on top of each other. He saw it was us, and he grinned. "Hey, strangers."

We got out of the Jeep, Jeremiah rushing to take the top container from him. "Here, let me get that."

"Thanks."

I followed them through to the outdoor kitchen.

"How've you both been?" Paul asked. "You, Jeremiah—" He looked him up and down. "—look good. No more brushes with death, I take it."

He laughed. "No, thankfully."

I slid my hand along the small of his back. The truth was, Jeremiah did look good. Really fucking good. He was happy. His new office was a dream come true and he now had two other staff. Howard and Georgia were both young and smart, really driven, and they brought a great energy to the office. And they both admired Jeremiah a lot. They respected him.

It was an office full of weather nerds, but Jeremiah would come home buzzed instead of beaten. He also talked to his dad more than ever. We'd been to Melbourne three times, and his dad had been back to Darwin twice since that first time.

He also had a stellar fucking sex life, I might just add.

So when Paul said that Jeremiah looked good, he wasn't wrong.

Derek came out of their tent, the closest to the kitchen. "Thought I heard voices," he said. "Welcome back."

We all shook hands and said hello, and ten seconds later, Jeremiah and Derek were off, looking through Derek's telescope.

"How's he been?" Paul asked quietly. "No problems?"

They knew all about the possible long-term health and medical complications that came with being struck by lightning. Some took months or years to develop, like cataracts and organ complications.

"None, thank God. He's been great. Passes all his physicals with flying colours."

"And how is he with storms now?"

I nodded. "Better. He still won't go out in them. Can't say I blame him."

"But he's here," Paul offered. "To go camping at the bunker for a week in storm season."

I chuckled. "Yeah. He still loves storms. And he still

studies the data. He's just safer about it now which, to be honest, is a good thing. No more crazy shit." I sighed. "I ain't gonna lie, a week of no interruptions, no work, no prying family, just us, one bed, and a storm every afternoon? He's not passing that up."

I thought about telling Paul of my plans, my surprise for Jeremiah, but for some reason I didn't. Now would have been the perfect time—and I did want to tell someone—but the only person I really wanted to tell was Jeremiah.

Paul smirked with a cheeky twinkle in his eye. "Yeah, about that. When I said he looks good, honestly, if it were possible, I'd say he was pregnant. He's glowing."

I laughed loud enough that Jeremiah and Derek both turned to look at us. "Well, we keep trying," I said, rubbing my belly. "Both of us."

Paul threw his head back and laughed. "But not for the lack of trying."

"Absolutely not." I gave him a nod. "And you two?"

Paul looked out to where Derek stood, and he sighed, a serene smile on his face. "We're great. He's great."

We both stood there smilin', like two fools in love.

"Oh, look at this," I said, taking my phone out. "We had some visitors last week."

I showed him the photos of two adult magpies on the patio railing with two adolescent chicks. "Someone got himself a family."

Paul looked at the pictures, then at me. "No way! Is that the bird you were looking after?"

I nodded. "Mr Percival."

We'd left his cage on the balcony, like Jem had suggested, with the door open so Mr Percival could come and go as he wanted. His days away got longer until it was a few days at a time that we didn't see him, then even longer.

But last year he'd come back with a friend, like he was bringing his girlfriend home to meet his two dads.

And then this year, there were babies.

"That is the coolest thing," Paul said.

"Yeah, it's pretty amazing. Jem was stoked."

"Might be time to take the plunge and become dog dads, or cat dads."

I snorted. Maybe . . .

"Speaking of taking the plunge, got everything organised?"

His grin was back. "Yep. Not much to organise to be honest. And you guys booking in, it was perfect timing. We really do appreciate it."

"It's our privilege." I clapped him on the shoulder. "Tell me what needs to be done."

***

THE MINISTER ARRIVED BEFORE SUNSET, AND AT THE EDGE of the ridge, overlooking the vast wetlands below, the sky a glorious palette of pinks, oranges, and yellows, Jeremiah and I stood witness to Paul and Derek's wedding.

I couldn't help but stare at Jeremiah as they talked of

love and forever, as they vowed to love and cherish each other for all their days.

Jeremiah in the fading pastel sunlight was one of my favourite sights in the world. Wet Jeremiah, and hot and sweaty Jeremiah, and turned-on Jeremiah were also my favourite kinds of Jeremiah.

Even the mad Jeremiah and annoyed Jeremiah.

I loved them all.

But there, against the most beautiful backdrop, stood the most beautiful man. Sure, Paul and Derek's wedding was lovely, but damn . . .

Jeremiah.

"I do," Paul said, making me pay attention.

"I do," Derek echoed, softly kissing Paul. "For now and forever."

And then, just like that, they were married.

Jeremiah and I both clapped and hugged them, and after the minister had gone, we ate seafood from the grill and drank champagne and toasted to the night sky.

But lightning flashed far out on the horizon as storm clouds moved in, and I could feel Jeremiah's nervousness rolling off him. I took his hand and pulled him toward our tent. "We're gonna head in," I said to Paul and Derek, but they didn't care.

They were too wrapped up in each other, slow dancing under the stars to music only they could hear.

Once we were inside our tent, I put my hand to Jeremiah's cheek. His face softened under the fairy lights. "You okay?"

He nodded. "Thank you for understanding."

I kissed him softly. "Any time."

He put his forehead to mine. "It was a beautiful ceremony."

"It was."

And god, I wanted to tell him.

It was right on the tip of my tongue, and my mind burned knowing that little box was right there in my duffle bag.

Should I tell him now?

I could . . .

But no. I wanted to be at the bunker.

Jeremiah ran his finger down the side of my face. "You sure you're okay?"

I nodded. "I am."

"You sure? Because I'm tired and I wanted to fall asleep with you inside me," he murmured. "But if you're not up for that . . ."

I barked out a laugh and took his chin between my thumb and forefinger. "Oh, I'm up for that."

THE NEXT MORNING, NOT LONG AFTER SUNRISE, I LEFT Jeremiah in bed and went in search of breakfast and found Paul and Derek in the kitchen. Derek had Paul pushed up against the counter and was sucking on his neck. He didn't even stop when he saw me. He simply smiled.

Paul laughed. "Morning."

"Yes, it is," I said. "Don't stop on my behalf. I'm just here for some . . ." I opened the fridge. "Food."

"Are you leaving this morning?" Derek mumbled, his mouth still on his husband's neck.

I snorted. "Yep. Soon as Jem wakes up." I took some fruit and yoghurt and clapped Derek's shoulder. "If you're not around, we won't come knocking to say goodbye."

"Good," Paul mumbled, and when I got to our tent, I turned back to see Paul was now facing Derek, his hands on his face, in a deep kiss.

I was smiling when I went inside, and Jeremiah grumbled at me from the bed. "You weren't here."

"Morning, sleepyhead," I said. "I was getting you some breakfast. Paul and Derek are putting on a bit of a show in the kitchen. We should probably leave."

He sat up. "Oh. A show? Any good?"

I laughed. "Didn't you have enough last night?"

He shook his head and fell back onto the bed. "Never, apparently."

I peeled the lid off the yoghurt, added a spoon, and handed it out for him. "Eat up. We have to get down the ridgeline."

He took the yoghurt and sat up again, frowning this time. "Oh yippee. My favourite wild pig track. Nothing like a vertical descent down the mountainside to wake me up."

I peeled the banana and pretended to deep throat it before I licked the length of it. "I have plans for you this afternoon, so hurry up and eat."

He stared at the banana, then shook his head. "Using promises of sex as a bribery tool is incredibly manipulative."

I bit the banana. "But it's effective. Now eat."

Half an hour later, fed and showered and packed up, we were back in the Jeep. Paul and Derek were nowhere to be found, so we didn't get to say goodbye, but I did beep the horn on our way out.

And down the side of the mountain we went.

Jeremiah only swore and gave me the stink eye a few times, and soon enough we were pulling up at the bunker.

He was smiling now.

He really did love it here. The seclusion, the ruggedness of it. That it was basic and rudimentary essentials and nothing else.

We got the side walls up and I checked for any uninviteds. I made sure the shower and toilet were frog-free, and Jeremiah gave everything a bit of a clean.

By mid-afternoon, it was stinking hot and we were both shirtless and sweaty, and he looked as happy as I'd ever seen him.

Maybe this was my favourite kind of Jeremiah . . .

We had one laptop monitoring the weather, and we did bring his new automatic weather station. He also wore his watch and we'd brought the chest strap, strictly for medical reasons, but he wasn't wearing it.

He was looking at the weather radar, and I was lying on the bed, tryin' not to think about what I needed to show him, wondering when would be the perfect time. Was there ever a perfect time?

Every time I thought of it, my nerves buzzed around in my chest like a box full of bees waiting to explode.

"There's increased storm activity about to hit," he said. "Lightning activity likely."

I sat up. "We'll be okay here, Jem."

He nodded, though that line between his brows told me he didn't really agree with me.

And then he started pacing.

I stood up and went to him, stopping his pacing with a tight hug. "You know you're safe here, and you've been in electrical storms since. Wanna tell me what's really bothering you?"

"Nothing."

I took his wrist and looked at his watch. "Uh, your stress beacon here says otherwise."

He grumbled. "I hate this watch."

I pulled his hips flush with mine and held his gaze. "We had storms here last year and you were fine."

He frowned again but wouldn't look at me. "I know. I just . . ."

"Jem," I said, chasing his gaze until he looked at me. "What are you worried about? Tell me."

"I'm not worried. I just . . ."

"You just what?"

"Paul and Derek," he whispered.

"What about them?"

"They got married."

"They did, yes," I said.

I would have smiled if he didn't look so serious. Thunder boomed in the distance and it startled him.

I tightened my hold and gave him a bit of a shake. "Babe, what's the matter?"

"Did you ever think it was possible?" His eyes

searched mine. "When you were younger, growing up. Did you ever think getting married was something that would ever happen to you?"

"Sure."

He deflated. "Well, yes. You're bisexual. It was always possible for you." He shook his head and tried to pull away. "Forget it."

I held him even tighter. "I won't forget it. This is clearly bothering you. And honestly, what the hell? Whether I married a guy or a girl. Whether I was gay, bi or straight, why does that matter?"

His eyes searched mine and he sighed. "I'm sorry. That was . . . I shouldn't have said that."

More thunder rumbled across the sky, closer this time.

"Jem, I always pictured myself with someone forever. Like my mum and dad. I always wanted what they have."

"I never had that. I never saw what that kind of love was like." He shook his head. "Even when I fell in love with you, it never occurred to me that it was possible for me. Not even knowing we were going to be witnesses for Paul and Derek." His lip pulled down, sadness filling his eyes. "Until I saw you standing there, smiling at me. And I thought . . . maybe. Maybe that was something we could do now."

Oh hell.

Oh fucking fuckity fucking hell.

He put his hand to his forehead. "And maybe that was something you might want to do? With me? One day. It doesn't have to be now."

Thunder cracked overhead and Jeremiah turned to the storm. "Do you mind? I'm trying to have a moment here!"

I burst out laughing and sat him on the bed. "I want to show you something," I said. "And tell you something."

I went to my duffle bag and took out the box that had been burning a hole in my brain since I got it in the mail, and I went to my knees in front of him.

"A month ago, after we'd booked in with Paul to come here and he called me back to ask if we would be the witnesses to their wedding, I spoke to your dad. I called him . . ."

"My dad?"

I nodded, nervous as hell. Those bees in my chest were really trying to break free. "I told him I'd been thinking about asking you to marry me. I wanted him to know. I wasn't asking permission, as such, but I did want him to feel included and to remind him that he wasn't losing you." I let out a breathy laugh. "And he went all quiet and I thought for sure he was gonna say no. But he said he was surprised it'd taken me this long. And he offered me this."

I held up the box, but Jeremiah was stuck staring at my face.

"Jem?"

He startled. "Oh, I'm sorry, what? Did you . . . did you ask my father?"

"I did. I've been thinking about this for a while, and well, Paul and Derek kinda beat me to it, and I didn't want you to think I was just asking you because of them. It just kinda gave me the push to do it. Anyway, your dad sent me this."

I offered him the box again, and this time he took it. "What is it?"

It was an old jewellery box. "Open it."

He lifted the lid and stared at the ring. He blinked quickly a few times before his eyes found mine. "Tully."

"It was your mother's wedding band," I said. "Your dad thought you might like it. He said you had your mother's hands, but if it doesn't fit, we can get it resized. If you want." He was stunned, clearly. He stared at me, then back at the ring, but he still hadn't said anything. "Or not. It's okay if you—"

A tear rolled down his cheek. "This is my mother's?"

I nodded.

"Oh my god, Tully," he said, a shaky hand over his mouth as more tears fell.

"I'm sorry. I didn't mean to upset you."

He laughed through his tears and took the ring out of the box. Then he handed it to me and offered me his left hand.

"Is that a yes?" I asked.

"You technically haven't asked me anything."

I snorted. "Jeremiah, will you marry me? Say you'll be with me forever. That we'll come here forever, to this place. That we'll chase storms forever. That we'll love each other and protect each other forever."

He nodded with more tears and a laugh, and I slipped the ring on his finger. It was a tight fit. "Oh, you might have trouble getting that off," I said.

He shook his head. "I'm never taking it off."

I stood up and pushed him back on the bed, following him so I could kiss him. His legs went around me, and I kissed him, our tongues in a familiar tangle, his hands in my hair.

As the storm raged on outside, as rain lashed the walls and thunder rumbled low and deep, he made love to me. Slow and deep, he slid in and out of me, taking me to that place only he could.

And when I was close, when my body was at the precipice, he froze. So far inside me, to the hilt, his eyes wide, and he licked his lips. "Lightning. Taste it with me."

He crashed his mouth back to mine, giving me his tongue as the sky outside lit up with a symphony of thunder and lightning.

Just for us, the storm played on. Cymbals and drums, lights and song. Music only we could hear.

As it would for us, forever.

THE END

THE STORM BOYS SERIES

Thank you for reading Tully and Jeremiah's story!

Outrun the Rain

Into the Tempest

Touch the Lightning

Go back to where it all began with Paul and Derek?

Second Chance at First Love

THE STORM BOYS SERIES

ABOUT THE AUTHOR

N.R. Walker is an Australian author, who loves her genre of gay romance. She loves writing and spends far too much time doing it, but wouldn't have it any other way.

She is many things: a mother, a wife, a sister, a writer. She has pretty, pretty boys who live in her head, who don't let her sleep at night unless she gives them life with words.

She likes it when they do dirty, dirty things… but likes it even more when they fall in love.

She used to think having people in her head talking to her was weird, until one day she happened across other writers who told her it was normal.

She's been writing ever since…

ALSO BY N.R. WALKER

Blind Faith

Through These Eyes (Blind Faith #2)

Blindside: Mark's Story (Blind Faith #3)

Ten in the Bin

Gay Sex Club Stories 1

Gay Sex Club Stories 2

Point of No Return – Turning Point #1

Breaking Point – Turning Point #2

Starting Point – Turning Point #3

Element of Retrofit – Thomas Elkin Series #1

Clarity of Lines – Thomas Elkin Series #2

Sense of Place – Thomas Elkin Series #3

Taxes and TARDIS

Three's Company

Red Dirt Heart

Red Dirt Heart 2

Red Dirt Heart 3

Red Dirt Heart 4

Red Dirt Christmas

Cronin's Key

Cronin's Key II

Cronin's Key III

Cronin's Key IV - Kennard's Story

Exchange of Hearts

The Spencer Cohen Series, Book One

The Spencer Cohen Series, Book Two

The Spencer Cohen Series, Book Three

The Spencer Cohen Series, Yanni's Story

Blood & Milk

The Weight Of It All

A Very Henry Christmas (The Weight of It All 1.5)

Perfect Catch

Switched

Imago

Imagines

Imagoes

Red Dirt Heart Imago

On Davis Row

Finders Keepers

Evolved

Galaxies and Oceans

Private Charter

Nova Praetorian

A Soldier's Wish

Upside Down

The Hate You Drink

Sir

Tallowwood

Reindeer Games

The Dichotomy of Angels

Throwing Hearts

Pieces of You - Missing Pieces #1

Pieces of Me - Missing Pieces #2

Pieces of Us - Missing Pieces #3

Lacuna

Tic-Tac-Mistletoe

Bossy

Code Red

Dearest Milton James

Dearest Malachi Keogh

Christmas Wish List

Code Blue

Davo

The Kite

Learning Curve

Merry Christmas Cupid

To the Moon and Back

Second Chance at First Love

Outrun the Rain

Into the Tempest

TITLES IN AUDIO:

Cronin's Key

Cronin's Key II

Cronin's Key III

Red Dirt Heart

Red Dirt Heart 2

Red Dirt Heart 3

Red Dirt Heart 4

The Weight Of It All

Switched

Point of No Return

Breaking Point

Starting Point

Spencer Cohen Book One

Spencer Cohen Book Two

Spencer Cohen Book Three

Yanni's Story

On Davis Row

Evolved

Elements of Retrofit

Clarity of Lines

Sense of Place

Blind Faith

Through These Eyes

Blindside

Finders Keepers

Galaxies and Oceans

Nova Praetorian

Upside Down

Sir

Tallowwood

Imago

Throwing Hearts

Sixty Five Hours

Taxes and TARDIS

The Dichotomy of Angels

The Hate You Drink

Pieces of You

Pieces of Me

Pieces of Us

Tic-Tac-Mistletoe

Lacuna

Bossy

Code Red

Learning to Feel

Dearest Milton James

Dearest Malachi Keogh

Three's Company

Christmas Wish List

Code Blue

Davo

The Kite

Learning Curve

Merry Christmas Cupid

To the Moon and Back

Second Chance at First Love

Outrun the Rain

SERIES COLLECTIONS:

Red Dirt Heart Series

Turning Point Series

Thomas Elkin Series

Spencer Cohen Series

Imago Series

Blind Faith Series

Missing Pieces Series

FREE READS:

Sixty Five Hours

Learning to Feel

His Grandfather's Watch (And The Story of Billy and Hale)

The Twelfth of Never (Blind Faith 3.5)

Twelve Days of Christmas (Sixty Five Hours Christmas)

TRANSLATED TITLES:

ITALIAN

Fiducia Cieca (Blind Faith)

Attraverso Questi Occhi (Through These Eyes)

Preso alla Sprovvista (Blindside)

Il giorno del Mai (Blind Faith 3.5)

Cuore di Terra Rossa Serie (Red Dirt Heart Series)

Natale di terra rossa (Red dirt Christmas)

Intervento di Retrofit (Elements of Retrofit)

A Chiare Linee (Clarity of Lines)

Senso D'appartenenza (Sense of Place)

Spencer Cohen Serie (including Yanni's Story)

Punto di non Ritorno (Point of No Return)

Punto di Rottura (Breaking Point)

Punto di Partenza (Starting Point)

Imago (Imago)

Imagines

Il desiderio di un soldato (A Soldier's Wish)

Scambiato (Switched)

Tallowwood

The Hate You Drink

Ho trovato te (Finders Keepers)

Cuori d'argilla (Throwing Hearts)

Galassie e Oceani (Galaxies and Oceans)

Il peso di tut (The Weight of it All)

FRENCH

Confiance Aveugle (Blind Faith)

A travers ces yeux: Confiance Aveugle 2 (Through These Eyes)

Aveugle: Confiance Aveugle 3 (Blindside)

À Jamais (Blind Faith 3.5)

Cronin's Key Series

Au Coeur de Sutton Station (Red Dirt Heart)

Partir ou rester (Red Dirt Heart 2)

Faire Face (Red Dirt Heart 3)

Trouver sa Place (Red Dirt Heart 4)

Le Poids de Sentiments (The Weight of It All)

Un Noël à la sauce Henry (A Very Henry Christmas)

Une vie à Refaire (Switched)

Evolution (Evolved)

Galaxies & Océans

Qui Trouve, Garde (Finders Keepers)

Sens Dessus Dessous (Upside Down)

La Haine au Fond du Verre (The hate You Drink)

Tallowwood

Spencer Cohen Series

GERMAN

Flammende Erde (Red Dirt Heart)

Lodernde Erde (Red Dirt Heart 2)

Sengende Erde (Red Dirt Heart 3)

Ungezähmte Erde (Red Dirt Heart 4)

Vier Pfoten und ein bisschen Zufall (Finders Keepers)

Ein Kleines bisschen Versuchung (The Weight of It All)

Ein Kleines Bisschen Fur Immer (A Very Henry Christmas)

Weil Leibe uns immer Bliebt (Switched)

Drei Herzen eine Leibe (Three's Company)

Über uns die Sterne, zwischen uns die Liebe (Galaxies and Oceans)

Unnahbares Herz (Blind Faith 1)

Sehendes Herz (Blind Faith 2)

Hoffnungsvolles Herz (Blind Faith 3)

Verträumtes Herz (Blind Faith 3.5)

Thomas Elkin: Verlangen in neuem Design

Thomas Elkin: Leidenschaft in klaren

Thomas Elkin: Vertrauen in bester Lage

Traummann töpfern leicht gemacht (Throwing Hearts)

Sir

THAI

Sixty Five Hours (Thai translation)

Finders Keepers (Thai translation)

SPANISH

Sesenta y Cinco Horas (Sixty Five Hours)

Los Doce Días de Navidad

Código Rojo (Code Red)

Código Azul (Code Blue)

Queridísimo Milton James

Queridísimo Malachi Keogh

El Peso de Todo (The Weight of it All)

Tres Muérdagos en Raya: Serie Navidad en Hartbridge

Lista De Deseos Navideños: Serie Navidad en Hartbridge

Feliz Navidad Cupido: Serie Navidad en Hartbridge

Spencer Cohen Libro Uno

Spencer Cohen Libro Dos

Spencer Cohen Libro Tres

Davo

Hasta la Luna y de Vuelta

Venciendo A La Lluvia

CHINESE

Blind Faith

JAPANESE

Bossy

PORTUGUESE

Sessenta e Cinco Horas